A RUTH... MC NOVEL

CHELSEA CAMARON

RYAN MICHELE

1st edition published: July 19, 2017

Editing by: Asli Fratarcangeli

Proofreading: Silla Webb

Cover Design by: M.L. Pahl of IndieVention Designs

This book contains mature content not suitable for those under the age of 18. Content involves strong language and sexual situations. All parties portrayed in sexual situation are over the age of 18. All characters are a work of fiction.

This book is not meant to be an exact depiction of a motorcycle club but rather a work of fiction meant to entertain.

****Warning: This book contains graphic situations that may be a trigger for some readers. Please understand this is a work of fiction and not meant to offend or misrepresent any situations. There is quite a bit of violence so if that's not what you're looking for then please don't read.****

Jessica Ham—thank you for your excitement and love of our books.

To every reader who embraced Ruthless Rebels MC and their second chance romances, we thank you!

CONTENTS

JOIN US!

Come join Chelsea Camaron and Ryan Michele in our groups on Facebook

Chelsea Camaron
Ryan Michele

Want to be up to date on all New Releases? Sign up for our Newsletter

Chelsea Camaron
Ryan Michele

SCHOOLED
(A RUTHLESS REBELS MC NOVEL 4)

Waylon “Triple Threat” Thorne–the untouchable.

Man of steel with a capital S.

His crystal blue eyes are something dreams are made of down to the way he carries himself, everything is beyond reality.

My first lesson in heartbreak. What happens when we both learn we’ve been schooled in miscommunications?

Chelsea Camaron and Ryan Michele have teamed up to bring you an explosive new MC romance that will have you panting for more of the Ruthless Rebels. Hold on tight, it's going to be a wild ride full of action and suspense that these two authors are known for. Throw in two people who finally get their second chance, and things are about to get smoking hot.

CHAPTER 1

THE ROAD TO HELL IS PAVED IN FUCKED UP SITUATIONS!

Jessica

Inhaling deep, the moldy mildew burns my lungs.

I look around me once again, the four walls are yellowed from time and lack of care. The only light peeking in comes from a one-inch gap on the top of the lone window that's now boarded up tight. The wood from the frame is still embedded in my hand from my attempt to remove the plywood from the window and find a way out. Ghost pains from a long since healed wound flare where the wood lodged in too deep and then the infection set in. It was agony. All because I tried to escape her.

I close my eyes.

"I'm nothing but trouble, Jess. You really need to walk the fuck away," Waylon's voice plays in my mind. "You're everything I ever dreamed in a woman, in a lover. Baby, I can't do it. I need to walk away."

He says this often, and I remind him we'll get through like always. "You're the strongest person I've ever met, Waylon Thorne, we can make it work," I plead, letting my heart overpower my mind. We're too perfect, too connected. He can't leave me.

"I'm weak, Jess. If I were any kind of good man, I'd kiss you one last time and never look back. I'm a selfish fuck to lay in this bed, my cock still inside you knowing I can't have you, I can't have this."

He begged me not to get tangled up in him, but I couldn't. He always told me he needed to leave me, and I always pulled him back in. Every time he said goodbye and told me not to call again, I always did. The love between us was too special. We were young. Too young, too wrapped up in each other, and too naïve to understand the path that lay ahead in our lives, but being together–I just knew we could do it. I pushed him to try, to stay, to throw away his past and believe in what we could be. My chest burns, the pain of my emotional scars cuts deeper and feels worse than any torture the woman holding me can ever cause me.

I hear the sounds of footsteps coming down the hall. Light patters telling me exactly who is coming. Automatically, my body tenses and my every sense shoots into alert mode. I lay still, steady my breathing, and keep my eyes closed but not tight, rather relaxed feigning sleep.

There was a time when every noise had me on alert and the fear of the unknown would suffocate me. Thankfully, things are pretty routine now and I don't have to wonder what is next … it's always in the back of my mind, but it isn't nearly as bad as it was.

The most damage done has been to my spirit. I always tell myself if I keep my mind out of her warfare then I will survive this.

The twists and clicks of the three locks being undone can be heard easily through the silence surrounding me. The doorknob squeaks as it turns, and the door creaks on its hinges as it opens allowing a sliver of light to shine through.

One. I count in my head. I hear her steps and regulate my breathing. Sometimes this makes things go faster because she doesn't have the time or the patience to deal with me. I don't know which, but I'm always grateful for the reprieve.

Two. Focusing only on staying relaxed, I fight my instincts. Another day, press on.

Three. The fight inside me left a long damn time ago. This is survival.

I keep counting to myself and keeping things even, steady.

Four. Everything in my life is methodical now. I don't live, I exist.

Five. Silently, I lay in wonder … what will she be like today? Which personality will she show me?

"Sweetness, it's time we give thanks to the Lord and have our breakfast." Her voice is soft, but high pitched so even a whisper sounds like nails on a chalkboard.

I remain steady, unmoving from my spot on the bed. Breakfast, that means morning. A new day that I can't keep track of. Once I resigned myself to not being able to escape, I stopped trying to sort out what day it was. Maybe I can sleep this day away and the next, and the next.

She sighs. "Heavens above, why must they anger us so? Spare the rod and spoil the child."

Before I can think about her words or react, hot liquid hits my t-shirt covered torso. The burn causes me to cry out, and my body jolts.

"I hate when you make me do these things, sweetness."

Pain. Shock. Revolt. I want to vomit. Tears threaten to leak out, I push them down, not about to give her the satisfaction even though the heat and possible burns are intense. She broke pieces of me a long fucking time ago, but I'll never let her see it. No, I tried being honest, vulnerable, she still kept me chained. The only power she will know she has is physical. Emotionally, I will not let her see me fall.

Slowly, I push myself to sitting, the shackles on my ankles feeling heavy as I move not allowing me to go too much farther than against the wall that is my makeshift headboard. Muscles I once had are no more. I don't get enough to eat to sustain attempts at working out even if I had a way to do so.

"There, there, I knew you weren't asleep, sweetness."

Time hasn't been well to my captor. Her once dark hair is now a stringy gray. Her face is covered in wrinkles and worry sets around her eyes. Her eyes though, they haven't changed over the time I've been there. They are still as cold as shards of ice that could cut deep into one's soul.

I lost count of time long ago. When the walls around you are the same, one day turns into five before you can even sort your shit out and keep any kind of track. Now, they all blend together only the small flash of light in the window telling me if it's day or night. Time doesn't matter anyway because it bleeds over and over like an open wound that never heals–never ending.

She places the plate on my bed with scrambled eggs, toast, an apple, and no utensils. The coffee now on my stomach won't be replaced, and I'll be left with only the hope she'll bring water sooner rather than later. Inside, I calm my nerves and know I have to behave in order for her to stay partially sane. Some days I can fake sleep, she will turn and let me be—other times this is the price I pay. For me, for that small reprieve—it's worth the risk—

worth the pain.

Over time, I've pushed her too far, testing the waters, and paid the price. Escape is not an option. Death will be my only escape. I just haven't found a way to make it happen yet.

Using sheets, clothes, and everything at my disposal to choke myself has left me sleeping on a bare mattress instead of not breathing. Drowning myself in the tub only left me with supervised showers and bathroom time—

which is beyond degrading. Starving myself would be more painful than the life I live and isn't an option. I'm afraid she would catch on and shove the food down my throat or worse, start some crazy IV and inject shit in me. The withdrawals when she finally stopped drugging me were bad enough the first time, I don't want to endure that again.

"Sweetness, it's time for our prayer and morning devotion," she instructs before dropping to her knees at the side of the bed.

Like a child, I clasp my hands together and bow my head knowing once this is over there is a good chance she will leave me be. Solitude is my only comfort in this life.

I wasn't raised in her faith, her religion, but like a mother, she's taught me as her child what she expects. There are many things that will set her off, not acting appropriately for devotion, prayer, or any bible lesson are without a doubt a trigger. It's something I won't win, ever.

She begins and I focus, knowing if I tune her out and miss something I will pay the price, painfully. "Father, we thank you for this day. We thank you for your many blessings and our time together, Jessica and I. We are patiently waiting for the day you return our sweet Waylon to us." She pauses as the emotions consume her. "Forgive me for failing and the Devil in his brother, Whitton, for taking him from us. Forgive me for not protecting our child, Father." She begins to sob like she does every single day we go through this.

I don't understand how a mother can give birth to two children and view one as evil and one as good. How can she even live with herself knowing she sees one of her own children as vile? It's something I don't think I'll ever understand. I used to ask her, and all she would tell me was it was shown to her when the boys were in her belly, she was given a prophecy.

Silently, I send my own prayer. After all this time, I have learned her bible. I have my own views on faith. What she has is beyond comprehension.

God, if you are real, please keep Waylon safe and away from here. If it's your will that I continue to endure this at the hands of his mother to keep him safe, I will do so with grace, humility, and the heart of a servant. No matter what happens, I beg of you to answer this single prayer: keep Waylon out of her life, out of her grasp, and let him have a life of love like he once gave to me.

My own tears fall as my heart shatters once again.

"Sweetness"—his mother reaches out and squeezes my hand. Her touch is like a scaly snake, but I refrain from flinching—"I miss him, too. You need to know, I thought he would return for you so much sooner. I thought our life would be different. The Devil has ahold of our boy, we must pray in earnest."

Hold it together, Jessica. He's stayed away this long, so my prayers are being heard if I'm to believe the religion she has thrust in front of me at every turn.

Bowing her head, she continues to pray, "Father, we seek forgiveness for our sins. When you find it in your heart to return him to us, we will do everything to hold him here, and at all costs we will keep Whitton from his life. This we ask in your Holy Name, Amen."

My stomach rumbles loudly.

"Eat up, sweetness." She pushes the paper plate toward me before reaching out to wipe the tears from under my eyes. Each touch is like acid, only burning my soul not my body. "I miss him, too. The bible tells us Jesus will return one day. Waylon will return, sweetness. We must have faith."

Standing, she moves to the door. Surprisingly, she doesn't turn the light off this time and leaves. The sounds of locks clicking into place are all I can hear as I pick up the paper plate with a shaky hand.

Is it bad I feel for her? Her twisted belief is wrong. She has everything so wrong. She needs help. The kind I know I'm incapable of giving her. All I want is for Waylon to stay safe and one day find my own escape.

CHAPTER 2

THERE IS NO SUCH PLACE AS IN TOO DEEP IN THE BATTLE OF GOOD VERSUS EVIL!

TRIPLE THREAT

"Didn't give you that intel for you to take off like a fuckin' lone wolf," Thumper barks into the phone at me. He's pissed, and I expected it.

"Can't have Skinny anywhere near her," I give back honestly. She'll kill him. I know it, he knows it, and she damn well is praying for it. "Keep him and Roe safe. Let him have this, I'll be fine." I wait for Thumper to argue.

He pauses. I know this can't be easy for him. He has treated Whitton and me as his family since we rolled into Granville, Alabama. After a life tossed back and forth from our mother's custody to fosters homes throughout Georgia, we landed with the Browns'. Not long after graduation, it was necessary we leave because our mother was hell bent on making everyone we were close to pay.

Leaving was hell, but staying was not an option.

Thumper's voice interrupts my thoughts, surprising me with his reaction. "I get it. Sometimes, we got shit we gotta do on our own. One call, one text, hell one fuckin' bat signal in the sky and you got the Rebels at your back, son."

The word burns deep in my soul–son. Thumper and Lurch have been the only father figures Whitton and I have ever had. Twin brothers, we've been together since conception. The pain my brother has endured at the hands of our mother … it's unspeakable.

All because of me.

Feeling the beast inside me rising, I head out for a run. At six-feet-seven-inches tall, I'm intimidating by most standards. I don't give a fuck. The park I stop at has monkey bars, and I begin pull ups until my fingers are numb and my biceps feel like they may bust.

As soon as Thumper gave me the name of the contact, the meet time and place, I took off. The hundreds of miles from home isn't enough distance to keep Whitton out of this. Yes, I know my twin and club brothers would stand beside me, behind me, hell in front of me, but this … this isn't about the Ruthless Rebels Motorcycle Club. No, this shit is as personal as it gets. This is my vengeance—my contribution to my brother and the motherfucking world. I won't fail this time. Waylon won't be here to stop me. He didn't want it on my conscious. What he doesn't understand is each day that passes with her still breathing burns at my soul. That kills my conscious to know what he went through, and she's still free of it all.

I need a fight, bust something, hurt something.

Muay Thai, a controlled martial art that, in history, gave warriors the ability to kill a man in a hand to hand atmosphere. It takes diligence, endurance, and balls of fucking steel. I have them all. The Browns', a foster family my brother and I lived with when we finally got taken away from our mother for one of the many times, got me started. The first time I landed my ass in the principle's office in grade school, Mr. Brown said I needed an outlet. He found me one at a local martial arts gym. Master Yung took me under his wing and gave me the balance I was seeking. Rather than kill my mother physically, I just did it over and over again in my mind.

For years, I trained. Fight after fight, underground and legit, I let the beast out.

Rarely can anyone match me to spar. It has caused me to lose many partners because they tire of losing every time. I found another outlet when we left Georgia.

If I can't find a fight, then I need to find a range and shoot some shit. Trying to free myself from the guilt I carried about Whitton's scars, I joined the military at eighteen. As soon as we left Georgia, I enlisted to break any connection MaryRuth, our mother, would have to us and the people who mattered. Whitton should have stayed back, but he didn't. He followed me, it was his duty. My brother's keeper—he knew I was reckless and took that role as my keeper as his life mission. I've never been alone. Whitton has always been with me.

The military was one line he couldn't cross, though. Apparently, when our mother burned his face, she caused permanent, unrepairable damage to his vision. Labeled unfit for duty, he was cut before he could begin. When I joined he always did his own thing in my area—odd jobs and shit, but there was a distance between us because he wasn't by my side through basic training. My time in service only gave me more control and more skills—like shooting. Master marksman, sharp shooter, I excel through the scope. I did my time and got out because being separated from Whitton had me distracted and on edge.

My brother's keeper … it has a magnitude of meaning. I don't know if he's mine or I'm his or we're just some tangled mess of the two. I just know that if anything happens to my brother, I'll never fucking be the same.

Ever.

Something has to give inside me before I get to Lambardoni. He will expect me to be a calm, cool, and collected player in their underground game. Thumper made the contact, scheduled the meet, and will expect me to handle myself as a Ruthless Rebel—not a half-cocked, pissed off, fucked in the head man seeking vengeance on his mother. The Lambardoni family has a deep history and mafia roots that keep an open trade from both their enemies and allies alike. Even as they move from one generation to another in charge, it's all seamless. Their control is never shaken from the outside looking in.

Family.

They believe in the blood bond. The beautiful Catarina and Kiera, daughters to the kings of corruption, are cherished, protected, and fierce in their own rights.

Our paths don't often cross. When they do it is business, always business.

This time, for me, it's personal. I'll give my marker knowing Thumper, nor a single brother in the

Rebels, will stop me when it's called. It's our code, their code, and pretty much a silent acceptance amongst anyone of our kind.

Tomorrow is the meet. Tomorrow I get the information I've been seeking for far too long.

I should wonder how my mother crossed paths with a top crime family. I should wonder what I'm really getting into here.

I don't.

Truth is I fear no level of pain, death, or dismemberment. The only thing to shake me is my brother. He's safe and sound in Alabama living the life he was destined to have with his woman, Roe. Knowing this, having comfort in this, I don't give a shit what she's tied herself to. I don't care if I live to see another day as long as my one-way trip to hell has her in tow.

My mother went underground two years ago. The leads ran cold. We don't know where she went or who she's been with. Whitton didn't want it on either of us when we had our chance to kill her, what seems like a lifetime ago. For all my brother has endured at that woman's hands, he called me off and I stood down for him. For a while, I kept tabs on her just to make sure she stayed away from us. Then she simply disappeared.

When Whitton and I first patched to Rebels, Thumper spread the word far and wide for anyone with any information on MaryRuth Thorne, the Rebels would pay cash for this intel. Only a few weeks ago, Val Lambardoni reached out, according to Thumper. Except it's not the money he seeks.

Val is a wild card in the Lambardoni family business. He's not the face of the organization, but not one to hide out in the shadows either. No, he is a well-known playboy with the women and a ruthless killer when tasked with the job. He's trained in martial arts, finance, and a perfect smile that really could be a damn toothpaste commercial.

I don't take him, his family, or his information lightly.

There isn't a doubt in my mind if he feels disrespected, he'll gut me on the spot. If he even thinks there is one ounce of me that doesn't take him seriously, he will issue enough pain to get my attention. It's the life he leads. I would expect nothing less.

One more night, then I meet the man face to face. He will share what he knows, and I will give my marker. Thumper already offered cash to which Val Lambardoni laughed and reminded my club President that, in his world, money doesn't hold near the weight of power. He has all the money he could ever spend in this lifetime or the next.

What he doesn't have … well, that is yet to be determined. This is why many men just like him call a marker. For the unknowns, the unexpected, and the what ifs of it all.

I understand it.

I give into it.

My word, my deed, my honor, and by creed, if Val Lambardoni ever beckons for my assistance, no matter what the cost, I'll be there … all for the opportunity to find my mother and put shit to rest once and for all.

Everything comes in threes. I'm a triple threat, and for my mother I'm glad to be judge, jury, and fucking executioner.

CHAPTER 3

OHANA! THE MEMORIES OF FAMILY AND HAPPIER TIMES BRING ME PEACE AND CAUSE ME STRIFE!

Jessica

"Father, we thank you for the many blessings you have given our family." She begins our morning devotion kneeling beside the bed while I sit up, head bent and pretend to listen.

Family.

It's a nail in my heel puncturing through. I miss my family. How long has it been? Have they given up? What day is it? Does it really matter?

Early on she would have me call my ohana, my family. With a gun to my head, I had to pretend to be busy and happy all the while scared to death either my mother or father would listen to me die.

Lying to my father while he is in Hawaii and I am God knows where in the states only killed me more inside. He'd always been a stickler for truth and loyalty, stating *without that you have nothing.* When one has no choice, even those morals and values are pushed aside for survival.

When was the last time I saw sun besides the small sliver of the window?

Growing up as a child on the islands, we praised the sun, worshipped our life, and the many things provided to us by the land and sea. My mother and father met when my mother took a trip to Hawaii at seventeen-years-old with her classmates. Quickly falling in love, she ended up staying rather than returning home to her family. In turn, she lost their support and contact.

For my father, it was worth it. Even when things didn't work and she left Hawaii for Georgia, she always said the love they had was something she would never regret. They never divorced, neither of them ever actually moving on.

He wouldn't leave the islands. She longed for the mainland. I spent my time divided. Until high school, when a tall boy with a perfect smile captured my attention. Then staying in Georgia was more important than going back to my father. It crushed my father a little, but he said he understood citing that I was just like my mom.

Every day I look in the mirror, I have my father's golden complexion, his dark hair—but mine has waves—dark eyes, accented with my mother's lips and round cheeks. I look like any hula dancer in a show but being away so long, I can't feel the ocean in my soul like I did as a child.

Rough waters cause too much unease in the depths of our being, my grandmother would say.

I no longer feel the calm of the sea or the tumble of the waves. I no longer hear the roaring of the ocean, or feel the salt in the breeze. Even when I moved back to Georgia from the islands, I felt it and I continued to worship it by spending time outside, knowing that somewhere my father was feeling the exact same sun. Now, nothing.

Numb.

My life is surrounded in a dark cave.

She moves beside me getting my attention back to her and the Bible in her hands. "Today's devotion, Jessica, comes from first Timothy chapter five, verse eight."

I stifle my groan. She is going to take this scripture, this passage, and contort it into something vile. This is not what God intended for his believers—surely, not.

"But if any provide not for his own, and specially for those of his own house, he hath denied the faith, and is worse than an infidel." She carries on while I try to seek some emotion inside myself other than loss. "I provide for you, for us, Jessica. When Waylon returns, he will care for us. God will show him the light; he will guide his path to us. We must be patient. My boy will not be an infidel. My boy will be strong for us."

She never talks of Whitton coming with his brother. It's always Waylon who is her son and Whitton, if mentioned at all, is evil. I don't want Waylon to find us. Is it sad? I worry Waylon can't save me, not without sacrificing himself.

I'm smart enough to know once she has her son back, she'll kill me. I'm certain, I have sinned in some manner where she will deem me unpure for her son. It will be a convenient excuse to be rid of me and have nothing in the way of her obsession with her precious baby boy. I'm simply a pawn in her sick plot to serve Waylon up on a platter to her God on high. Once she no longer needs me, she will dispose of me.

"Speaking of family," I say barely above a whisper, "should I call my father soon?"

"Oh, I've text him. He thinks you've been abroad traveling Europe."

The slight hope I allowed myself to feel is gone in an instant. A girl like me, in this position, shouldn't have hope. I know better, but I have so many questions. How does she continue to pay my cell phone bill? I know she leaves every day for some time, but I don't know if it's long enough to work at a job. We have this place, electricity, water, food, but I have no idea how she pays the bills and keeps people away from here—at least I haven't heard anyone.

My mother has stopped answering my calls and texts because my cousin got married—my best friend, Amelia, and I didn't attend the wedding. This was a while ago, and the last time we spoke she was so angry with me. That's what twists in my head whenever I think of her. She thinks of me as a spoiled, entitled child who wasn't raised to be as I have become. The disappointment is one my mother doesn't think she'll ever get passed, those were our last words. Lucky for the woman holding me, not for me, though.

How can someone so sick in their mind be so fucking smart? She has kept everyone from reporting me missing. None of them have looked deeper into my words when we talk to even question why they haven't seen me in so long. They have commented on the change in my voice, the lack of excitement even when I've said I was doing such fun things, yet my mother, nor my father, have sought me out. Now, really nothing. The last time I spoke with my father he sounded distracted. The distance was crushing. My mother … she hasn't answered in so long I quit trying.

It's heartbreaking.

The only hope I have left to be saved is that this woman's precious God will take her home to Heaven soon. He can take me first. I've made peace with my sins. I worry with her age, mental state, and lack of health consciousness that she will pass and no one will find me, and I will die a slow, painful death chained to a bed. The flip side of this scares me more than my death or hers. Because otherwise, it comes down to Waylon being my saving grace in all the darkness here, and I don't want him here to suffer like I have.

My love for him has withstood this test of time. As much as I should hate him, I don't. I should pray for him to give her what she wants so I can be free, but I don't. No, I want Waylon to have a life without her. Happy. Free.

Being born to this level of crazy is not something anyone should have to endure. He's found his escape, and I pray he keeps it.

Why she chose me, I still don't understand. Waylon and I broke up years before I was taken. He felt it was best. Last I even knew of him, he joined the military. Whitton followed, but I don't know that he actually joined or just went where his brother did. Just before I went off to college and then later MaryRuth took me away, the rumor in small town Georgia was the Thorne boys found themselves in a motorcycle gang.

Honestly, I don't care where Waylon is as long as he stays far away from his mother. She's sick, twisted, and I can't even figure out what she wants from him, but it can't be good.

I close my eyes and still remember the moment vividly.

With my tan legs tangled around his cream skin, I find myself almost purring. "Waylon Thorne, you have awakened something inside me I didn't think was real. You're my fairytale come true," I croon in bliss after spending a night making love to the man of my every dream.

He sighs and shifts, pulling me over him. His hands come up to cup both sides of my face. "Love is pain, Jessica. Don't forget this. We're in too deep. The pain you will feel in the short term will lessen in time and be far easier than the pain if you stay. I'm black inside. The fairytales you wish for, you deserve. You are a beauty beyond compare."

Before I can register what he's saying, he rolls me over so I'm under him. His lips hit mine. Hard, raw, rushed, he devours, claims, and shares. With every touch of his tongue to mine, he's giving and taking, and it's all too much.

Abruptly, I feel the loss of his lips, his body, and I rise up to find him standing, dressing rapidly, and avoiding my eyes.

"Love is pain," his voice is strained. "I never should've fallen for you. I never should've tangled you with the evil inside me. You're free of me, Jessica Hokulani Quemuel."

Those were his parting words without ever looking back.

I look up to the ceiling and count the cracks. Like when I was a little girl and would pluck petals from a flower saying, "he loves me, he loves me not," I do the same with the cracks. "He'll be okay. My sacrifice is worth it." My eyes go to the next one. "This is a losing battle where we're all gonna die," I whisper to the nothing around me. Crack by crack, I do the same sentences over and over.

Love is pain, Waylon Thorne. A lesson he taught me so well, and he doesn't even know how deep that pain runs.

I can only hope and pray he never learns.

CHAPTER 4

IF ONLY THIS WERE A MOVIE AND NOT FUCKING LIFE!

TRIPLE THREAT

It's fifteen minutes till six. The small restaurant is dark. The booth in the back corner is the seclusion necessary for the kind of conversation we need to have.

I take my seat. The waiter comes over, a tall dark haired man in a white button-up shirt, black dress pants covered in a black half apron, and black tie; he doesn't smile, he doesn't greet me. He places the wine glass in front of me and pours the deep red liquid to a quarter full. I don't move to take the glass. While wine may be considered dignified or maybe even tastes like heaven with the meal, I don't plan to indulge.

"Mr. Lambardoni will be with you shortly. Once he arrives, your food will be served."

"Good fuckin' deal, but the food isn't necessary," I chime back and pick up the glass of ice water in front of me beside the wine glass.

Before I can say anything else, the waiter disappears just as a dark haired Italian man in a crimson button-up shirt strides up. His face matches the picture, and his build matches the description I was given. Val Lambardoni slides into the booth across from me, not introducing himself or bothering with casual pleasantries. I don't even make a single move to stand to greet the man; he doesn't seem interested either.

Good.

This is business.

"The spaghetti carbonara is the best in town. You must eat, Mr. Thorne."

"Lambardoni, we both know what I'm here for, so cut the small talk. The Italian in you may wish to eat until we bust while we buzz off some wine, but me I'm a beer and chicken wing kind of man. You have information I want; I have a marker in return. Let's get to it."

He steeples his hands together on the table. "While I respect a man with brutal honesty and find your frankness to be refreshing, we need to be clear on some things. You already know it's not money I seek. I have more than I can spend in a lifetime. As for a marker, while those are invaluable, I have my own associations where I may never call on you. So let's eat, let me determine your skillsets so that I can feel comfortable in sharing what I know and what you may do for me in the future. For a marker unused is a waste, and a man I can't trust is one I can't use."

"If you trust anyone in business then I'm afraid, Lambardoni, my marker is one you shouldn't call upon, because I'll damn sure never trust you. The lifestyles we lead may be different, as you have yours in a suit and office while mine is an open road and leather. We're both in a situation that allows for zero mistakes. Trust no one, consider that my free advice."

I move to stand when the man rolls his head back laughing. I raise a brow in question.

"Best fuckin' answer ever! Sit, eat, drink, the information is here." He reaches into his back pocket and retrieves an envelope he slides to me. "You see, a man who actually could think for two seconds I would trust him is the kind of man I don't want to do business with. The man who thinks he has my trust, thinks he has some power, and in this game of fucked up life, never let a single motherfucker have power over you."

I take the envelope and hold it in my hand. The weight miniscule in physicality but overbearing in the power it contains.

"You know how to reach me when the time comes to call your marker. Until then, you enjoy your meal, your night, and whatever the fuck else you do."

I slide from the booth without caring about casual pleasantries or expectations. I don't care how the mafia handle their business. The man can choke on his pasta, marinara, or whatever the fuck he's eating. Hell, he can choke on pussy for all I care. I need to get back to my hotel, sort the information in this envelope, and devise the plan that ends my mother for good.

As I crank my bike and ride off, I feel this pressure on my chest. The same crushing pain I felt as a boy listening to Whitton fight back pain every single time she fucked him up.

Mark him, she would say. She had to mark him so *they* would know. It was so everyone could see he was tainted when he wasn't—not one single bit.

How could our mother see me so perfectly and him so disgusting? How can she see good versus evil in her twins?

My brother, he just took everything she put on him. Every pain, every stone she threw verbally and physically, Whitton took it all.

I did, too.

I took it in a different way, but I'm just as scarred as him. His you can see, mine you can't.

Seeing Whitton with Roe is a balm to my bleeding soul. Finally, he has peace, a happiness, and a real love.

I knew love once.

Jessica Hokulani Quemuel, her Hawaiian middle name, meaning divine star, was everything pure, right, and good. I'm everything ugly, dirty, and bad.

I left her in a bed the day after putting enough money in her bank account to get her on her feet. It was everything I had saved. I let myself get lost in her. I let myself feel. Years later, after getting hooked with Thumper, getting my patch and my cut of the money, I again made a deposit to her account. This time it was enough to buy a house, car, and carry her bills for a few years.

Only, the money hasn't been touched.

Jessica had more power over me because of my emotions than anyone in my life—including my brother. Knowing what my mother was capable of in the name of love, I had to let her go. I had to keep Jessica safe.

No one will ever have that hold on me again. It killed me to walk away, but it was best for her and me.

With my emotions pushed back down, I pull in to my parking spot in front of the cheap ass hotel I'm crashing at for the night. Sitting on a hard ass double bed with a stale smoke stench assaulting my nose, I open the envelope ready to end this once and for all.

The information in front of me has me asking more questions than finding myself with actual answers.

MaryRuth, now using the last name Castle, works at a nursing home in Wilmshurst. She has been there for almost two years, exactly the amount of time she disappeared off our radar. She rents a two-bedroom house down the street from the facility. The card I hold has an address, phone number, and a list of her accommodations for working at the nursing home. All of it's a bunch of shit. My mother can be whoever she wants at any given time as long as it suits what she wants.

Although there is no indication that she has family, there is word from her co-workers that she has a daughter, who she speaks of often, which is probably just her warped mind making shit up.

The picture of MaryRuth Castle is unmistakably my mother, but with a lot more wear and tear. It seems as if life hasn't been kind to her, which is a blessing. Mrs. Brown always talked about karma and how actions went around and came around. With a small bit of hope, my mother has felt that pinch even just a little.

Why she's using a different last name is beyond me. Except she might be worried my brother and I will come after her and kill her. Whitton told her the last time she attempted to stab him, that if she would let him be, he would do the same and therefore spared her life.

He did this knowing it was me who wanted her dead, but I wouldn't break his word. The bond we share is deep, but there is a time when it may need to be broken for the better of us both.

Well, brother, you have a woman now. I like Roe. More importantly, I like Roe with Whitton, so to protect her I'll do anything necessary—like kill my mother.

Whatever this woman has going on, she better brace herself because I'm coming for her. And this time it's to put an end to looking over my shoulder and to give my brother the freedom, happiness, and love he's always deserved.

CHAPTER 5

MEMORIES ARE AN APPETIZER BEFORE A MEAL GOES TO SHIT!

Jessica

I fight to stay asleep, to stay in the dream. Closing my eyes, I keep my mind where I want it. The night I met Waylon Thorne.

"I can't believe your parents let you have a party while they're out of town!"

My friend, Phoebe, looks at me and wiggles her eyebrows. "Well, they don't exactly know. Live it up while we can, Jess." She squeals before tossing back another Jell-O shot. "Help me make the PJ in the bathtub."

"Wait! What?" I ask, not having a clue what she's talking about.

"Look, my sister went to a frat party, she swears this stuff will taste like Kool-Aid, but if you eat the fruit, it will be sweet and fuck you up. So, I cleaned the tub yesterday and used my mom's shower this morning. Now we gotta take the cut up strawberries, pineapple, oranges, apples, and kiwis and dump them in the tub together. I paid my brother by doing his paper for school to buy us the alcohol. We have a keg he's bringing in an hour. We just need to dump the Everclear, Vodka, and Sprite into the tub with the fruit. After we get that mixed so the fruit absorbs

mostly alcohol, we'll add the fruit punch and ice just before everyone comes."

"I don't know about drinking out of a bathtub."

She slaps me on the shoulder playfully laughing. "Everclear is like hundred-fifty proof. That alcohol level will kill anything that could be dangerous to us."

I sigh. "And kill our livers, too; but hey, who needs those."

The afternoon passes quickly into the evening as the party starts and escalates into a madhouse of drunken teens.

I am sober.

I don't know why I thought this would be for me. It's not. Spending my time divided between the islands and Georgia, I guess I just wanted to hang out with friends. I don't have many of those.

As people set down cup after cup of the bathtub concoction and the beer, I find myself cleaning up behind them as much as I can. I round the corner in the backyard to check on Phoebe. I see her being held in the air by two guys with a third holding the keg tap forcefully to her mouth.

She's thrashing her legs, but they hold her up while her hands are on either side of the keg. I see beer spew from her mouth.

She's choking.

I panic. Just as I rush over, I'm bumped by two girls I don't know kissing and groping each other. I lose my balance and tumble straight into the pool.

I swim to the top, my lungs burning for air. Just as I reach the side of the pool, two hands grab me and lift me up. I'm placed on my feet and my eyes roam upward until they settle on the fiercest of stares I've ever seen.

"You okay, beauty?" his deep voice rumbles.

I can't hold back. I blink back the emotions. Oh Waylon, I'm not okay and never will be. If only I could close my eyes and go back to that night again. Know what the future holds so I could have warned us both.

The locks to the door turn as I brush the tears from my eyes quickly then look at the crack for sunlight. Only a small glimpse of the light peeks through telling me that it's time for our evening devotion.

"Sweetness, it's shower time," she says, entering the room carrying a key in her hand. The key that unlocks the cuffs at my ankles, but it's what's in the other that keeps me on point. The gun. The weapon I have no doubts in my mind she will use on me without thinking twice.

I can't remember the last time I bathed and judging from my stringy hair, it's been a while. Growing up, I'd love to stay under the spray and watch the water flow down the drain taking the days with it and only leaving me clean. Now, showers are the most degrading thing imaginable. I'd say I hate it, but I hate everything about being here so it's moot.

"Up you go," she instructs, and I swing my legs as far over as they will go. She waves the gun at me. "Don't get any ideas, sweetness. I wouldn't want you to miss Waylon's return." My stomach roils, and I hold on to that small bit of hope that Waylon will stay far away from here.

She unlocks the cuffs, and I set my feet on the hard plank wood of the floor. It feels so foreign, not having stood in days or weeks—I'm not sure. My knees buckle as I try to stand putting my weight on them, and I crash back to the bed.

"No playing around, sweetness." Her words turn dark, and I force myself together. I rise, but it's on shaky legs. "Move it along," she orders, and I shuffle my feet through the door, down the small hall, and into the bathroom. The only thing on the walls are pictures of Waylon, more like a shrine. A large picture of him in the middle with his life scattered around him. Along with crosses and tacked up pieces of paper with verses from the Bible.

Once, I looked. Now, I keep my head down because seeing them only makes my heart hurt more.

The bathroom is as plain as you can get. Light blue tiled walls from floor to ceiling, a toilet, sink, and shower. There is nothing on the countertop, and the toilet paper is sitting on the back of the toilet. Like I could hurt her with the damn thing it sticks on in the holder. She is quite paranoid, but I've given her reason to, at least in the beginning. There was a time I fought. I lost each time until I have now resigned myself to this.

Inside the shower is a small bottle of shampoo with conditioner and a bar of soap. There is no curtain on the shower or glass. It is completely open.

"Shower now, sweetness. We have to do our devotion before bed."

Stripping out of my t-shirt and underwear which is all she'll let me wear, I climb in the shower as she turns the knobs. I jump as the freezing water hits me, but say nothing. She'll allow it to be a bit warm, but cold showers are a norm. No more standing under the really warm spray and enjoying the day washing down. No, this is a wash your body quickly and get out.

She sits down on the toilet seat, and I know my temperature is going to be frigid today, which sucks. She holds the gun up, aimed at me, as I quickly shower then turn off the water. I stand there shaking for several moments before she reaches down underneath the sink and grabs a towel tossing it to me. I quickly dry. Being watched while I do this is an invasion—it's humiliating, degrading, and downright disgusting.

But she never leaves me alone. Ever. Unless I'm locked in my room. My dungeon. My hell. She reaches back under the sink grabbing a clean shirt and underwear, and I put them on methodically, wishing I could have some pants or even shorts. It's a simple thing that many take for granted, but for me it would be paradise. Which isn't saying much.

"Let's go, sweetness."

I move back to my room, and she follows me as I enter the space that is my hell. As routine, I make my way to the bed, sit and she comes and shackles on the cuffs to my ankles. Only then does she set the gun by the door.

"Devotion time, sweetness."

Clasping my hands together while my wet hair dangles down, I listen to her ramble, twisting and turning scripture into what she wants instead of the actual meaning. After years of hearing the same things over and over again, the real meanings come through loud and clear.

After she gets done crying for Waylon, she rises. "Sweetness, get some rest." I say nothing as I watch her walk out of the room, close the door, and leave me in darkness.

Laying down, tears fall from my eyes. My life is not my own. It will never be my own again. Not until the good Lord takes me from it. But for some reason, he hasn't granted me that wish yet, but there is still hope. A small sliver, but it's there. It's all I have any more to hold on to.

Waylon always told me he was bad and I needed to stay away from him. He wasn't. Ever. He was my rock. He was my calm in a storm. He was my everything.

"It's gonna hurt." Waylon's weight pushes me to the bed. I've never felt so safe in all my life than I do in this moment, here, with him.

"I don't care," I whisper as his hard length brushes up and down my core sending shots of tingles through me. Waylon has given me several orgasms using his tongue and mouth, but we've never gone all the way. I've never gone all the way with anyone, and I'm ready.

Waylon kisses me, continuing to rock back and forth as his hands roam my body. The room becomes hot and my body on fire. He kisses down my neck, shoulder blades, my chest, nipples and makes a path all the way to my core where he licks me.

My hips buck up and he holds me down, rubbing me back and forth then inserting his fingers and driving me crazy.

"Let go, Jessica."

A flick of his tongue and a twist of his finger has me exploding. Light flashes behind my eyelids as I muffle a cry. Waylon carries me through still rubbing and petting until I fall to the bed, my breath coming hard and fast.

He climbs up my body, his lips attacking mine. I wrap my hands around his neck pulling him closer to me.

When he abruptly pulls away, I look at him confused. Then he reaches over and grabs a condom. I can't help but watch in amazement as he rolls it on his length. "You sure about this?"

"Yes," I answer as he comes back down over me. His eyes penetrating mine so deep he can see into my soul. One that is carved only for him. Forever.

"I'll go slow." He shifts his body, and I feel him at my entrance. He pops the tip in, and I feel my body stretching for him. In and out, in small movements, he inches his way inside of me. Each movement sparks new feelings inside of me as parts of my body that have never been touched come alive.

He halts. "It's time. Are you ready?"

I nod as he looks deep in my eyes not breaking the connection we have. He thrusts hard, and I cry out as the pain hits hard. He stills, unmoving his hips, but kissing my face and neck. "It's okay, baby," he coos in my ear, petting and taking his time.

It takes several moments before the pain begins to subside. It's still there, not completely gone, but it doesn't hurt as bad.

"I'm good."

His head pops up forming that unbreakable connection between us once again. I get lost in those eyes letting him see everything. How much I love him. How much I care for him. How I would do anything in this world for him.

It's what I see back that knocks me on my ass. It's the same. He loves me just as much. It's there, plain as day, as he thrusts inside me back and forth, his gaze not once leaving mine. The burn grows slowly all the while we're together in the moment. Loving one another.

As I come, my eyes stay open, but I clench my teeth as I watch him. When his lips come down on mine and his body jolts, only then do I close my eyes and succumb to the kiss.

The moment is beautiful. The moment is perfect. It's two souls connecting as one. An unbreakable bond that will forever be between us. A love so deep it's imbedding in our skin, heart, and souls forever.

I blink back the tears as they fall hard and fast, unable to stop them. Waylon and I had many times together when we made love, but that first time was the best. It was the start of us in an entirely different way. I loved him with everything I had. I still do. Even after all of these years. I do. I just pray I never get to tell him that.

CHAPTER 6

THINGS THAT MATTER: FAMILY, VENGEANCE, AND HONOR!

Triple Threat

Three weeks later

Another shithole town.

My mother sure knows how to blend in, find a poverty-stricken city and fall into life. The house is a run-down place with a graffiti-covered board blocking a window. The others have curtains blocking any view in. There are no lights on inside peeking through the cracks of the cloth, and the old Chevrolet Caprice sitting in the drive has seen better days or years.

Surveillance.

I have spent more than enough time mastering the skill of watching without being seen. Being here, but not.

Invisible.

Hours pass and no activity comes from the home. Not a single light flickers, a curtain moves, or even a shadow telling me that something or someone is inside, but unless my mother walked somewhere, she's in there.

Even as I feel the need to stretch, I don't climb out of the Toyota Corolla I bought for cash off a lot. The tint is a three percent visibility. The lower the percentage on a light test, the darker the tint. There is no way from any distance or even standing up close the average human eye will see into the vehicle.

After the purchase, I stripped the inside and assembled my weapons hold. With the pull of a fabric tab in the passenger seat, I lift the middle section of the seat and have access to two Glock nine mils and four clips—each secured in a padded hold. In the backseat, pulling down on the headrests opens a compartment that covers the backs of the seats, where I have two AR-15s, along with six magazines—half of them filled with two-two-three rounds and the other five-five-six rounds. The center console is securing two buck knives, while just resting in the door is a machete.

I don't know who MaryRuth has aligned herself with, so at this point, there isn't a measure too strong to ensure my safety. I know what the woman is capable of. I lived it. My brother lived it. She isn't to be taken lightly.

I will use my very last breath if necessary to make sure she's dead before I leave this city.

My phone rings, and I pick it up to see the caller ID.

Immediately, my gut twists with concern. "Roe, everything alright?" I answer with my first question rather than some generic pleasantry.

"Depends," she sighs, and I feel the panic rise.

"Roe, is Skinny alright?"

"TT, are you alright?" Instead of answering my question, she asks me her own. I notice there is no emotional inflection in her tone, there is no hint of crying. As much as that woman loves my brother, he's fine for her to be so calm on the phone with me.

"I'm fine, Roe."

She sighs. "We miss you, TT."

I still watch the house to my left, but there is a weird tightness in my chest thinking of Roelyn Duprey and my brother. I'm happy they found their way back together after so many years apart. She's the perfect match for my brother, was then and is now. The way she wants to have me around and involved in their lives has been soothing to know she doesn't want to separate my brother and me. She wants that bond. That family, and I like it just as much as she does.

"Miss you, too," I mutter honestly.

"I know what you're doing is for you."

"Roe," I warn her. "Don't get in my shit."

She clicks her tongue. "TT, you eat all the shit I cook. Who else can I get to choke down my tater tot casserole?"

Oh this woman, she's all things good that Whitton deserves. Since they got their own place, she's invited me over for every meal. I swear there are days Whitton says she thinks more of me than him. I sincerely doubt that's true, but I do know that having me around means something to her. When Roe and my brother first found their way back together, she was worried about me accepting her, liking her.

Truth is, there isn't one single thing I can find wrong with Roe. I just struggled and still struggle to be around her. She is like this ray of sunshine, this taste of citrus burst that is so refreshing, and I dare not taint it with my bitter shit. I had that once, and I left it behind for Jessica's own good. Whitton needs Roe so I can't walk away from her, but I can try my damnedest to keep her at arms length as much as possible.

"I mean really, TT, Skinny stays skinny because the man doesn't have the same love of cheese you and I do. Think tater tots smothered in a colby and cheddar cheese blend that you have to wrap around your fork like spaghetti, because it pulls so thick when you try to pull a bite off your plate."

I find myself almost smiling. "Get knocked up and your kids can eat that, Roe. Just make sure you don't clog all your arteries before you can have the babies."

"Not the same." She pauses, and I can feel the emotions come through the phone. "And you know I can't have a baby with you away. Your brother will be too freaked out something might go wrong. And the macho man he is won't tell me he's worried, but you'd be a good distraction."

She's right, and it pains me. Skinny isn't a man to talk about his emotions. Neither am I. Knowing he needs me and there is that possibility I won't be there—well, it kills. But if it's me who gets caught in a crossfire from my mother, so be it. Skinny and Roe will live on. She'll make sure of it.

"You two will figure it out when the time comes."

She pauses. "Triple Threat," she says somberly. "Waylon," she hesitates, no doubt expecting me to correct her. I don't. "I miss you. I know we haven't had time to get super close. But family is everything. I don't have much, but I have Whitton … and I feel like I have you as my brother, too. I miss you being over for dinner or just to share a beer. Even if you don't talk a bunch, you are part of our lives. I just wanted you to know, having you gone, well, things aren't the same. We'll be happy when you get home."

"Damn, woman." I drop my head against the headrest to the car. "Man like me ain't made to feel. Love my brother, love you for what you give him. No matter what shit I find myself in, Roe, you hold Skinny down."

I hear her hiccup in the back. "Please, TT, be safe and come home to us soon." Each word cracks with her emotions, and it somehow breaks through all the barriers I have built up over the years.

"Take care, Roe," it's all I can say before I click the phone off.

I study the house again.

The woman who gave me life is behind those walls. She's not full of the kindness, the heart, and the goodness that Roelyn has.

She is clouded in the evil she claims runs through my brother's veins. Well, MaryRuth, you're soon going to find out the evil you have tried to tame all of Whitton's life has been in me all along.

It's my mission to make sure my brother is safe to have his happy, this goodness, this sweetness with Roe for the rest of his fucking life. To have, to hold, and to cherish until his very last breath … I'll give it all to make sure he gets it.

CHAPTER 7

THIRTY-SEVEN BEERS ON THE WALL … NO, NO, CRACKS IN MY SOUL!

Jessica

The ceiling above me has thirty-seven cracks in it. Some large with the drywall open, while others are small cracks that could be fixed with a little bit of spackle. My heart longs to be a child again, to be with my dad one more time. My father worked with his hands all the time, building and creating.

He taught me how to fix a crack in a wall saying that *everyone needs to know how to spackle and fix the wall. You pay for that shit to get done all the time, you'll go broke.* He also taught me how to paint walls, trim, and ceilings. He tried to teach me plumbing, but the only thing I can figure out is drains.

In my old apartment, I fixed a leaky sink that my landlord would never touch. But toilets, I didn't catch on to because those stupid rings on the bottom of them. Seals, my dad called it, but I never got them on right and they leaked. We can't figure it all out, I suppose.

When I was younger, I thought I would get one of those fix-em-up houses and do all the repairs myself; or at least the ones I could do. It would be beautiful, old, and covered in thick dark wood trim everywhere. The home would be two stories, with bathrooms everywhere and I'd have a room. A large one, with windows all around it letting every bit of light in.

Looking around my cave, the darkness is almost maddening. It's a cyclone of despair eating at my insides every moment I'm here. Once I thought I was at my lowest point, where all I did was cry, but that wasn't it. This is it. Then I had hope. The tears that came were ones that still held that sliver of promise that I would escape this woman and this madness. She was dumb and naïve to think her family would come for her and hunt her down. Now, there is none of that. There is nothing.

The woman I once was has died and vacated my body. I don't even have the energy to miss her or crave her back.

When I first met Waylon, I was shy because he was so hot. But somehow, he took a shine to me. The more I was around him, the more the real me came out. He brought it out.

The more he believed in me, the more I believed in him. He was always honest with me. He always told me he was bad for me. I didn't understand it then. I do now. Only, it wasn't Waylon Thorne who was bad for me, it is his mother. He just couldn't see it then and probably doesn't now.

I had so many dreams for us and imagined our lives all the time.

There was no doubt in my mind that he was the man for me. Even being young, I knew he was everything I wanted. When he left me, my heart went with him. The money he left in my account sat there for a long time because I was angry he left it. Angry he put me in that position. The one where I felt like a plain whore in a way.

Then I had no choice but to use it. I felt this rush to get out of Georgia. I needed a fresh start. The thing about small towns, everything reminds you of what you once had. Waylon didn't even really explain things—he left, and that was it.

I thought the day he left and the many days after were the worst of my life. Roe, who was very wrapped up in Whitton, said he left, too. Waylon called, and they took off together.

Women scorned.

Except as much as Roe and I were in the same place, we weren't. I struggled to relate to her. While she was close with her mother, I was close with my father. A father I hurt terribly when I didn't return to Hawaii.

Don't get me wrong, there was a time my mother and I were close. We just never had the connection I had with my dad.

I was too young to deal with my emotions.

So, I ran.

It took some time, but I set up my life in Florida. Fort Pierce is a quiet town on the Atlantic Coast. I could have my toes in the sand after a long day at work. I spent my mornings taking classes at a local community college and afternoons serving food at a small seafood restaurant.

I was lonely, but surviving.

I thought the worst was behind me.

Maybe in some ways it was, but when his mother brought me here, the real pain began. My mind goes back.

The bar isn't crowded, then again, it's a Thursday night. Nervously, I flip my hair for the hundredth time. I'm waiting on my blind date, Paul. I've spent days chatting with him on an online dating site.

Part of me feels like I'm wasting both of our times. Just closing my eyes and thinking of my time with Waylon makes my body come alive. Why am I trying to move on when, clearly, my mind, heart, and body aren't on board with it?

Because it's been years, I mentally remind myself. He left me, not the other way around. He threw me away, tossed us away, like yesterday's garbage.

Taking a sip of the margarita in front of me, I relish the burn of the alcohol and remind myself this is a new beginning. Blowing out a breath, I take another drink and another.

The last thing I remember before it all went black is looking at my watch to see I had officially been stood up. When I woke up, I was in a hotel tied up. MaryRuth slapped me and began preaching about my impurity to meet another man when I was clearly destined for her son.

For three days, we traveled with me stuck in the trunk of some old Chevy car, my hands restrained at the wrists with zip ties and my ankles with duct tape. Every time she stopped she made me drink water before injecting me with something to make me sleep. Having no way to relieve myself, I spent days in my clothing that was soiled more than once.

It was degrading on so many levels.

At the time, I thought it couldn't get worse.

I was wrong.

Waking up, all I wanted was to have a shower and to puke. Whatever she had been pumping through me was clearly going to be my next test in survival—withdrawals.

I shake my head clearing out the memories. I can't go back there. I'm still here and need to focus on now. I survived it. I've survived her.

Footsteps.

The locks turning.

The door creaking open.

I don't pretend to be asleep. I don't even battle with my mind about what's to come next.

She stands there with the light behind her, my eyes blinking to adjust to the brightness. When she flips on the small light, I tear up just a bit, but hide it quickly. She's carrying a plate with a sandwich, chips, and carrot sticks and a cup.

"Time for evening devotion, sweetness." She sets the food down on the floor along with the cup, kneels and begins her prayer. I do what I always do, bow my head and place my hands together in front of me.

"Lord, we thank you for this beautiful day. One where we are a step closer in our wonderful Waylon coming back to us. Jessica misses him just as much as I. Patience is not something we should ask for, Lord, and we understand this now. We have learned. We are practiced, and we will wait as long as it takes for your will to be to bring our boy home. It's in these things we pray in your Holy Name. Amen."

She reaches down and pulls the food up to the bed. "Eat up, sweetness, it's time for bed. Tomorrow we will have our Bible lesson on contentment and seeking nothing more. For tonight, we simply pray and devote our day, our time, and our lives to having Waylon return."

I'd rather she leave, but I guess today she wants to stay. Unfortunately, I'm starving and devour my food quickly.

"That's a good girl, sweetness. Get some rest." She turns out the light, closes the door, and locks it.

I'm alone and reminded once again there is no way out. This wasn't what my life was supposed to be. But it's what I got.

CHAPTER 8

ADDICTED TO PAIN, IT'S A TRAP, BUT I DON'T TURN AWAY!

TRIPLE THREAT

I watch as the lights flicker on in the room with the board on the window, only a peek of it at the top. I look to the clock on the console and wait. It stays on for about thirty minutes, then flicks off. Thirty minutes in that room only. I look down at the small notebook and notice that no matter the shift MaryRuth works, she goes into this room at least twice a day based on the light showing through. A few other lights went on and off, but I could only see in the cracks.

Could it be her bedroom? I'm not sure. The light in the other room is on for much longer periods.

Leaving, I make my way back to the hotel and sit on the lumpy as hell bed. She's in that house, and I need to make my appearance a surprise. It's time to plot out a solid plan to get the job done so I can get out.

In order to have the plan and the energy to see it through to the end, I need rest. I'll crash here and gather my reserves. This shit is going to end by my hand and soon.

According to the information from Val, she works different shifts at the nursing home every week. She was home in the evening tonight, so that would lead me to believe she's mornings or afternoons.

The best plan I have with my mother is surprise, being in her home when she comes home from work unexpectedly. I need to nail down her schedule, so I'll get up early and survey the scene. Once I have the times down, I'll make my move. There is no out here. She will be extinguished.

Loud banging sounds from the door. I grab my Glock and make my way there on cautious feet. Looking through the peephole, my anger rises to explosive levels. I turn the handle and swing the door open.

"What the ever-loving fuck are you doing here!" I growl, grabbing his shirt and pulling him into the room, slamming the door and locking it. "How the fuck did you find me?"

Turning to him with my arms crossed over my chest, Skinny, my brother, and the main reason I'm here, stands looking around the place calm as can be. "Can see you spared no expense," he chuckles.

"Skinny, what the fuck are you doing here? How did you fuckin' find me?" I ask again, and something in my tone has his eyes finally coming to mine.

"They got an app for everything, brother." He holds up his smart phone. "Now, you wanna click the safety on that gun you're still holding and have a chat with your brother?"

"No," I bark back at him while putting the gun on the dresser.

"Now, fucker, I've missed you and this is the welcome I get. I have prime pussy at home in my bed, and I came to drag your head outta your ass to bring you home."

I shake my head in disbelief. "Skinny, walk out that door, get on your Harley, and don't look back."

"No."

He's as firm in his resolve as I am mine.

"Don't want you tied up in this shit."

He shoves my shoulder. "Fuckin' asshole, I'm as tied up in this shit as you are. I came out of that same cunt. You can't fight this alone. And I'm sick of Roe wanting to know when the fuck you're coming back. Swear to fuck, she worries more about you than me."

"Go back to Roe. Fuck your woman, hold her, love her, and forget where you ever came from, Whitton," I say his given name so he can understand how serious I am.

"Two years the bitch has been untouchable." He rubs the back of his neck. "You ever think there might be more at play here than we even know?"

"Don't give a shit. Whatever it is, I'll take it on."

He throws both hands up in frustration. "Be clear headed, brother. You ever think about the reason I don't push for her to be in the ground?"

"Don't care, Skinny."

"You ever wondered why?"

I shake my head because honest to God, I don't care.

"We never went to a normal church, Waylon." He tosses out my name knowing he will keep my attention. "Never. All those years, when she would dare take us out, we went to those weird buildings that had no windows—no natural light coming in.

First thing they did was separate us. What kind of people are okay with holding a little boy in a janitor's closet? But they did it in the name of God."

This time I shove his shoulder. "Don't you fuckin' justify her shit on some crazy ass mind fuck cult or even try to blame the Bible itself. MaryRuth is twisted and plenty of people believe, have faith, all that shit, and they don't do the shit she did."

"Just sayin', brother, what if she's not all we have to worry about?"

I hate when he's right.

"Food for thought," he adds as he walks around the room. "Let's get in that clown car you got sittin' out front and get some real food since you ain't got shit to eat here but some protein bars. I want a steak, fucker."

"You aren't gonna leave me to do this, are you?"

"Fuck no," he says, strolling to the door without a care in the world.

My gut churns. We're too close to her and together. This is a recipe for disaster, but he's as stubborn as I am. He's not going to leave.

Following him out the front door, I climb in the car and we drive to the grocery store where I park.

"You aren't gonna take me to a place where I can get a beer and get served a meal?"

"No, I'll get you a beer, some bread, bologna, and some chips. Make that shit work. I gotta sleep and find a way to get your ass back to Bama."

On a sigh, he clambers out of the car giving in. Scanning the lot, I don't see the old Chevy Caprice in the parking lot, so we should be safe.

We aren't in the store ten minutes before the hair on the back of my neck stands up just as we walk out. Just as we climb in the little Toyota, I hear an engine roar. Looking to my right where my brother is about to shut the door, I see the hood of the Caprice coming at us fast.

"Skinny," I yell just as I hear metal crunch and my brother cry out.

The car shakes around me, airbags explode. My head slams onto the door before it pops open, and I fall out onto the ground, the wind being knocked out of me.

I blink, dust from the airbags clearing. My vision is doubled before coming to focus to see MaryRuth stand over me with a gun.

"Waylon, my son has returned." She smiles and her eyes shine in pride.

Before I can knock the bitch on her ass, the gun fires and I feel the searing pain of the bullet hit my shoulder. She looks into the car; I lift my head to see Whitton slumped to the side. She fires again sending a bullet into his shoulder just beside his neck.

"Get up and get in my car before I give him another one to the head!" she orders me, and the green of her eyes flares telling me the evil inside her wants an excuse to shoot my brother again. He's unconscious, but I can see his chest move as he's breathing.

"Before you think of doing anything to me, you should know … I have Jessica!"

My mind spins. "What the fuck are you talkin' about? Who is Jessica?"

"Jessica, your Hawaiian—or do they say Polynesian beauty? She's been with me for almost two years, son. We're going to be so happy to have you home. She's going to give you beautiful babies, my son. We can raise them together."

The rage builds and I want nothing more than to gut her, but I need to know where she has Jessica. As much as I want to kill her right this instant, I have to be patient and sort out where Jessica really is.

Jessica. My sweet, beautiful woman. I wanted her to never be touched by any of this. Now my worst nightmare may have come true despite all my efforts.

Fuck, if she really has her … I try to stop the thoughts that run like a movie and hope the bitch is lying.

My critical mistake: not keeping tabs on the one person who truly brings me to heel.

Lesson fucking learned.

Jessica, I'm coming to set you free.

My mother holds the gun on me as I get into her car. The good thing is I can take her, even with a gunshot to the shoulder, blood oozing from the wound—I can take her. The only reason I'm letting her do this pony show is to get me to Jessica. My Jessica. The one I left to be safe from this crazy bitch.

It takes everything inside of me to tap down the rage festering in my soul. Instead, I fake injury wanting to catch her off guard as soon as we get into the house. Her neighborhood is shit, but I don't need other eyes.

"Oh, my Waylon, we're so happy you're home! We've prayed every day and night for your safe return. I just knew you would. Jessica will be so excited."

I have not one doubt she's telling the truth, and it sickens me that Jessica had to listen to her crazy rambles.

"How long have you had her?" I ask, hoping that it's recent, but even a minute is too long with my mother. The information I was given only gave me a location and current job for MaryRuth. I have no clue what she's been up to in the time she's been practically a ghost.

"Oh, we've been spending time together the past two years, son. Sitting and waiting for your return, and now you're here."

Two fucking years? No way—no fucking way she's had her that long. It just can't be. Guilt hits me hard upside the head. I should have looked. I should have known something was wrong when she didn't touch the money I sent. I should have looked into it. I left her to this. Me. The cause of her being stuck with a crazy woman.

"What have you been doing?" My voice pitches even though I shoot for calm. Right now, I just want information, as much as I can get before we pull up to Jessica's hell.

"Praying for you, son. Always praying for you."

I swallow the lump in my throat. "What else?"

"Well, you see, Jessica got a spot of the Devil in her and tried to leave our home. Now she spends a lot of time in bed."

I turn to face her seeing her leathery skinned profile. "What did you do to her?"

"She's fine. You know I wouldn't do anything to the woman who's yours. God set her on this path so she could bring you home. It's all part of the bigger plan, Waylon."

There had better be nothing wrong with her. I swear to God himself, I'll make my mother's death even more painful.

She pulls up to the shack of a house cutting the engine. My arm throbs, but it's nothing compared to the anger and adrenaline I have pumping in my veins.

"Out ya go. I'm so excited!" she cheers, covering the gun with her purse, stupidly, and handing me the keys. The woman is out of her damn mind. She honestly believes I'm going to be here with her.

Opening the door, a horrible smell comes from every angle. Garbage or rotting food, I don't know, but it's something strange. She slams the door behind me, tosses her purse to the chair, and aims the gun at me.

Not giving her one more second to think she's in charge of this, I reach out with my long arm and snag the gun just as it goes off grazing the side of my body. There's a burn there, but it isn't anything compared to the rage.

She gasps as if she didn't expect me to grab her gun and turn it on her. "Waylon!" she cries out, but I ignore her and hold the gun up aiming it at her head.

I reach behind me and pull out my phone hitting the buttons I've memorized.

"Yeah," Thumper calls from the other end.

"Skinny's down outside the IGA grocery store on Landford Road. Don't know if he's breathin', but I've got a situation where I can't be there. You got a man, because calling the cops is gonna get dicey."

"Yeah, on it. Got a marker I can call in, and we're on our way. I'll get someone on him, and we'll be to you in a matter of hours."

"Thanks."

I click off the phone needing to get this shit done. "Where is she?"

"I was just kidding, Waylon. I don't really have her." Her mind games are relentless. I remember them as a child, how she'd try to pin Whitton and I against each other. Wanting me to hate him just as much as she did; but I didn't, ever.

I walk up to her and move around the back of her pressing the gun to her temple. "Nah, I don't think you should get to go that easy." Holstering the gun in the back of my jeans, I grab the knife and put it against her throat letting her feel the bite of pain from it.

"Bitch, fuckin' tell me where she is," I growl, and my mother says nothing. "Now!" She jumps and the knife digs into her flesh, and blood drips from the wound.

"Down the hall."

I push her body in front of me. Several doors are open and looking inside, Jessica isn't there. The last door on the right though, the one where I clocked the plywood on the window, it has locks—fucking three of them.

"Unlock it!"

With shaky hands, she reaches in her pocket and pulls out a set of keys. Ever so slowly, she unlocks them.

"I did this for you," she says, and it only makes the knot in my gut grow tighter as she pushes open the door.

The blackness that is my heart crumbles and shatters as I see Jessica sitting on a mattress, legs shackled and only wearing a t-shirt. Her hair, her beautiful, long, dark, hair is stringy and brittle. Her round face once full of life is dull and shows despair. She's defeated. She's given in.

She is lost.

Holy shit, and this is because of me. All of this is because of me.

CHAPTER 9

SO MUCH FOR ANSWERED PRAYERS!

Jessica

The noise from the other side of the door caught my attention. Then I heard a pop like a firecracker, but there's no way those are in the house. Then voices, two of them and one sounds like a man.

An angry man.

Panic should fill me, but it doesn't. I know things can always get worse, but at this point, I can simply hope for death to take me away from this misery and still keep Waylon safe.

The locks turn slowly, and fear bubbles. I feel. I feel the panic and in the panic, I find hope. Why would she bring a man in here to see me? What is he going to do to me? She hadn't done anything sexual in all the time I've been here, but hearing the man's voice I can't help but wonder.

I sit up on the bed as far as my legs will allow and wrap my arms around my knees, pulling the t-shirt over to cover me. Fight or flight, my body prepares as my instincts take over.

The knob on the door turns, then opens. The breath I thought I took in leaves in a whoosh. Waylon stands behind his mother, and he holds a knife to her throat with blood already coming down her neck.

"Waylon," I whisper, feeling like an elephant sat on my chest. He's gorgeous and no longer the boy who left me in bed, then disappeared. No, now he's all man.

He's tall. He practically hunches around his mother. His shoulders are broad almost not fitting through the door. Blood covers his shirt.

He's hurt.

But his face shows no sign of pain.

No, in the depths of those blue eyes is hatred like I've never seen before.

His chiseled face is tense and full of fury.

MaryRuth squeaks, and I see his forearm flex as he maintains control over the knife in front of her neck. My eyes meet his.

I get lost. There was a time when I saw nothing but heaven and happiness inside him. This, this is a personal kind of hell.

He's looking at me. I'm looking at him. Time keeps passing.

"Our Father," MaryRuth whispers, and he cuts the knife deeper stifling her words.

He's standing at the door, eyes pinned to me. This has to be a shock to him as much as it is me.

His eyes change. It's stark, but plain as day. I had never feared Waylon even though he was a big guy, with big hands, never once was I scared of him. This moment. This instance, I am.

I watch in horror as the knife is torn across his mother's throat spurting blood everywhere as she drops to the floor in a heap, her eyes open and staring directly at me. I scream loud and piercing. I have never seen a woman get killed, nor a dead body before, and I could have made it through my whole life without it.

Waylon comes directly to me, envelopes me in his arms, and twists my body so I can't see the dead woman in the room. He cocoons me in his warmth. I should be afraid. Yet, I'm not.

I've lost all control and can't stop screaming, but not because of Waylon. It's shock from everything. My face feels hot as my pulse races.

Waylon is here.

He just killed his mother in front of me.

He is here to free me.

"Shh…you have to stop screaming. We can't call attention."

I breathe in and out hard feeling his body and strength surrounding me. I'm able to stop the screaming. It takes me a while, but somehow, I calm.

"Sonvabitch!" is growled from the doorway, and I move to see. More shock hits as Whitton stands at the door looking down at his mother. Blood covers his shirt, his face is swollen, and he has a wound on his neck that is still trickling blood. "I wanted information from her before she went to meet her God, asshole."

"Call Thumper. He's got guys comin' to you."

Whitton pulls out his phone and dials a number. "Hey, Jess." He looks at me almost casually. There is no shock, no surprise, just like this happens every day. Then again, Whitton has always been mellow. I never understood why he could be so okay, so settled in life, when his face shows his scars. I could tell in his eyes he was tormented by something, but never questioned it.

Part of me wishes suddenly I could go back in time and have a better friendship with both Whitton and Roe. We knew of each other and hung out from time to time, but it wasn't a close connection.

"Hey," I answer quietly, as Whitton steps out of the room talking on the phone.

"Do you know where the key is to the lock on your ankles?"

I shake my head. "No, she only unshackled me so I could shower. When she came in the key was always in her pocket."

"Skinny!" he bellows out, making me jump. "Sorry, baby." His words are like sweet molasses down my throat, warm and pure. Damn, I've missed him.

"What?" Whitton barks from the doorway.

"Keys for the braces on her ankles. Check the bitch's pockets."

Whitton looks down at his mother, disgust clearly written on his face, and I can't blame him. "Great. Leave me with the good jobs."

He shuffles through her pockets, dropping some loose change and a couple of clumps of lint, but no key. My heart squeezes, and I reach out to Waylon. "Please get me out of these."

"Need to search the house," he orders and begins to stand up.

I clutch him tighter. "No! Don't leave me in here by myself. Don't go." I'm full out panicked thinking that if he leaves this room somehow, some way, the woman on the floor will rise up and I'll be back where I started. She has her God on her side, at least in her mind, and heaven help me I can't endure anymore. I prayed for him not to come back, but now that he's here, he can't leave me. I can't lose him; I can't lose my freedom when it's so close.

"Breathe, Jess. I'm right here. Not goin' anywhere." He looks over at Whitton. "Search everything. Find it." Whitton nods and takes off.

"Thank you."

Tears spring to my eyes, and I allow them to fall rolling down my cheeks and onto my t-shirt. "What day is it? Year? I don't know how long I've been here."

"First, are you hurt anywhere?" he asks instead of answering.

"My ankles are raw and burn every once in a while. She put salve on them a few times, but I think they're okay. Other than my legs not working so hot because of laying here all the time, I'm fine."

He nods, obviously okay with that answer. "It's July nineteenth, two thousand seventeen." More tears spill over my cheeks.

"I've been here for years, Waylon," the words are whispered and crack as my emotions win over me.

He pulls me into his arms as I sob big racking tears at all the time in my life I've lost at the hands of that woman. She kept me locked up for two damn years. No wonder my family gave up. That's a long time.

"Got em'," Whitton calls, coming into the room.

I quickly wipe away the tears as Waylon shifts and Whitton sticks the key inside the lock. This time with the click of the lock, I feel relief.

"I need to stand," I say, quickly wanting to feel my weight on them and walk—right the hell out of this house.

"Slowly," Waylon advises, taking my arm and helping me to stand. My knees wobble and just as I'm about to fall back down to the bed, he holds me tight not allowing me to fall. Something he did for me all those years ago. New tears threaten, but I push them down and take a few steps.

I look at the dead body lying on the floor, her limbs a mangled mess and blood pooling around her. Hopefully, now, she can find her own peace—whatever that may be. "She was sick."

"Know that," Waylon responds instantly, still holding on to me.

"She thinks you're the next Jesus or God or something."

Whitton snorts. "Like that's anything new."

Waylon's body tenses. "It's not your fault," my words are matter of fact and precise. He just shakes his head, and I hate that he thinks all of this was is fault. The woman needed help. It's on her, no one else.

"Do you have anything here?" Waylon questions as we walk by his mother and out the door. He doesn't bother to look at the walls, and I'm thankful for that. He doesn't need that burned into his brain.

"My phone. She's been texting my dad who thinks I'm in Europe or some crap."

He looks down at me. “No shit?”

“Your mother was smart. She has my mother hating me and my father not caring that he hasn’t seen his daughter in two years when he knows I would have gone over to the islands for a visit by now to see him.”

“Hate to tell ya this, but that woman wasn’t that smart.”

“What does that mean?”

“Let’s find your phone and get you the hell out of here.”

He moves us into the living room, and the smell is atrocious. Luckily, whatever is in here didn’t seep into my room or I would have gagged to death. “I have nowhere to go, Waylon.”

Something changes in Waylon. His eyes shut down and the lines around his eyes disappear. It’s as if he’s void.

“Skinny!” I jump at his tone, cold almost like he’s not there two feet in front of me.

“Yeah?”

“Take Jessica to the hotel. See if our bitch mother has any clothes that will fit her and take her there so she can shower.”

“Why don’t you …” Whitton’s words are cut off by some sort of look that I can’t see because Waylon’s back is to me. Whatever it is, Whitton registers and lifts his chin.

“She’s got a phone here. Find it, and I’ll start clean up.”

Only then does Waylon turn to me and the pain is so dense in his eyes, I want to cry. “Told you I was nothin’ but bad, baby. I’m so fuckin’ sorry.”

With those parting words, he turns around and leaves me with his brother, taking yet another piece of my shattered, tattered heart.

CHAPTER 10

THE BURDEN OF BLAME IS ON ME!

TRIPLE THREAT

Walking back into the room Jessica was held captive, my entire body trembles. The mattress is filthy, covered in stains that I don't think, or at least I hope, aren't Jessica's. Nothing else in the room, except for the bolt attached to the floor and the chains that held her there.

Chained there. Like an animal. Like a nothing. For two fucking years.

What did she endure? Did my mother bring men here? Did she allow Jessica to be tormented?

Deep inside me the rage erupts like an explosion invading every muscle, cell, and blood vein in my body. It's an anger that I've never felt before, and I move over to my mother's rotting corpse and begin to kick her. Over and over and over again. Kick after kick—her body flailing lifelessly with each one. But I don't care. I want her to hurt.

I wish she was alive so I could kill her again. The slice to her throat was too quick for the shit she made Jessica endure.

Blood spatters my boots and jeans as I nail her in the throat practically taking her head off her body. Yelling at her doesn't do much, but it helps to get it out.

"You fucking bitch! I should have killed you all those years ago." Kick. "I shouldn't have listened to Whitton. You know the one you treated like shit and blamed everything on. Yeah, he's the motherfucker who wanted to keep you alive." Kick. Kick. Kick. "You deserve hell!"

Her body flies against the wall smearing her blood all down it. Only then do I catch my breath, but the rage lives on.

"I give my word, to your God, my God, and every fucker who can listen, if a single soul touched one hair on Jessica's body, it's now my mission to kill them all."

I heave deep breaths in and out. All control is gone.

I look at the mangled mess of my mother's body. "I'm fuckin' evil. You sick, twisted, bitch! Not Whitton. The evil's inside me!"

Hit after hit, I punch the wall. I relish the burn as my skin splits open. The sheetrock crumbles under the impact, I keep going.

A phone rings in the other room breaking my pattern of pounding into the wall. Moving to it, I pick the flip phone up and open it.

"Hell hath no fury," I answer on a growl.

There is a menacing laugh on the other end. "Well, if Waylon Thorne hasn't found his way home. It's the second coming of the Lord. Maybe your mother was right and the girl was the way to do it after all."

My stomach tenses. Jessica was used against me. I knew it, but this stranger confirming it only kills me more. "I'm no God, I'm not good, but I promise you, whoever the fuck you are, I'll send you to meet your maker like I did my cunt mother. NO. ONE. TOUCHES. JESSICA. AGAIN." The words come out clipped, terse, and with all the venom running through me.

"Oh, my son, I would only be so blessed as to be sent back to the Heavens by your hand."

The call disconnects before I can figure out anything else.

I let out a scream not caring who hears. Call the cops, call the therapists, lock me up. I don't give a shit. I'm in an unimaginable hell of my own making.

Charging through the house, candles with Jesus line the countertops and pictures of me are scattered throughout the place. Each one twisting my rage further. With a swipe of my arm, they all go shattering to the floor, breaking in thousands of pieces just like my life and being born to that woman.

Pictures line the walls with stupid notes that mean nothing. I pick them, one by one, off the wall and send them soaring across the room embedding themselves in the shitty walls.

Not holding back, I devour the living room, flipping furniture and smashing the lonely television. I lift the couch about ready to turn it over with the stench hits me hard almost knocking me down.

Lifting it, I slam the piece back down to the ground as a rotting animal caucus is underneath of it. It looked as if it were a dog, but with one sight of maggots over it, I couldn't look anymore. Why in the hell did my mother have a rotting dog in the house?

I heave in a breath trying not to pass out from the stench.

My phone rings, and I answer. "Yeah."

"Five minutes out," Thumper says, hanging up. Damn, they made good time. The phone call reminds me of the one I just received on my mother's line. It takes me a bit to focus, but somehow, I manage to search the kitchen, looking for what I have no idea, but something to tell me who this guy is.

Once the club gets here, I'll have a trace run to see what I've got on my hands because no name popped up on the caller id, so it wasn't in her contacts. But he sure as fuck knew who I was and who Jessica is, and more importantly, what the fuck my mother was up to.

I'll destroy him. Fucking annihilate him.

Maybe Skinny was right and we should have asked the bitch questions before I took her out. I couldn't help myself, though, seeing Jessica like that. I just needed it to end. I needed to take out the threat.

I needed to feel in control of something when everything was in chaos.

The door swings open, and I have my gun out pointed at it.

DJ and Thumper walk in. "What the fuck is that smell?" DJ says as greeting while hacking like he might puke, and I put my gun away.

"Dead dog under the couch," I reply, coming out of the kitchen and to them. "Bitch is dead in the other room."

"Brief," Thumper says, looking around the room his lip going up in disgust, from the smell or the scattered pictures of me on the floor I don't know.

I give him the low down on the situation including the phone call from the man just a while ago.

"Fucking shit. Nothin' like goin' out in hell," Thumper says as DJ moves through the house taking everything in.

"This bitch has a serious hard on for you, TT," DJ calls out. "My mom wasn't the posterchild of good parenthood, but your mom; damn, TT, she takes the cake on fuckin' crazy."

"No fuckin' shit, man." That's not even the half of it. "Place needs to be torched. No other way to get this shit taken care of."

"Got guys outside from the area, gonna take care of this shit. Anything you want from here?"

I glare at Thumper. "No fuckin' way."

"Good, go to your girl and we'll sort this out."

"I'm goin' home," I declare. "Not stayin' here a second longer unless you need me."

DJ walks in. "Then what the fuck are you gonna do about Jessica?"

"Skinny'll make sure she's good." She sure as shit doesn't need me in her life a second longer giving her any more pain.

"This shit isn't your fault," Thumper says, taking a step forward.

I take a step back. "Yeah, it fuckin' is. I got Skinny's extra set of keys. I'm takin' his bike and ridin' home."

"If that's what you need, brother." DJ's concerned words only have me needing to get out of there more. This is exactly why I don't talk about my shit to anyone. It's my shit and doesn't need to be on anyone else's shoulders.

DJ went through some shit back with his woman, Kenderly. His own mom got her tangled with the wrong kind of men. Her mother was grieving, and Kenderly was doing all she could to pay the bills. DJ's mom ended up getting their house blown up. In the end, it gave Kenderly and DJ a chance to sort their shit. Those two are happy and have a baby now.

It's good to know he got his peace. Skinny's got Roe. Jessica, well, she should hate me after what she's endured because of me. It's not a look I can handle ever seeing in her eyes.

The pressure, the emotions, it's all too much. I need to be alone.

I study the men around me, the men I trust and look up to. Yes, it's all too much. I don't deserve the kind of life they have been able to build for themselves.

"I'll see you back at Rebels." I get the fuck out of here needing the air, freedom, and space to ride.

CHAPTER 11

FREEDOM NEVER FELT SO BAD!

Jessica

Whitton is quiet as we make our way to the hotel. I have to ride in the backseat of a wrecked Toyota Corolla because the passenger side doors aren't able to be opened. I see a little notepad sitting on the passenger seat with scribbles of words. The door is caved in, and the air bags sag inside the vehicle.

Every time we have to stop or Whitton has to make a move, I watch him grimace in pain through each movement.

"What happened to the car?" I ask, wondering how hurt Whitton and Waylon really are.

"My mother happened," he says plainly, without emotion.

My mother, the simple title carries so much weight. While his mother was awful and hurtful, my own was not. I can picture her light brown hair, creamy skin, and green eyes like it was just yesterday since I saw her last. She thinks I turned my back on her for this life of travel, luxury. How can she ever understand the truth?

Whitton pulls into a hotel that isn't the fanciest of places, but it's not a creepy looking spot that you can rent a room by the hour either. Then again, anything is better than the hell I've been in. I'd rather be out on the streets under an overpass than there again.

"Let's get you inside and cleaned up, Jess," Whitton says, and I see his eyes roll back a bit.

"You okay, Whitton? Someone I should call?" With the blood on him and looking at the car, he really needs to go to the hospital. Although that would certainly call for questions. Ones I don't really know how to answer.

"Nah, been shot before. Just crashing off the adrenaline of wakin' up and my brother bein' gone. Took me a few minutes of searching shit in the car to figure out where the fuck he was. Just glad to get there, he's safe, you're safe. The rest of the shit can heal."

He leads me inside. The temperature is cool. I see no signs that Waylon has even been here.

"Do y'all travel often? It's like no one has been here."

"We do when the job calls for it. Talk for another day, Jess. I'm gonna grab the bag from the trunk. I don't wanna put you in our mother's clothes so I'll get you one of my shirts and pants to put on. I'd offer some clean boxers, but I'm a commando man, so maybe TT has some."

I raise an eyebrow. "Who is TT?"

"Triple Threat, TT, is Waylon. It's a road name. Another conversation for another time, Jess. You go get cleaned up."

Tears threaten to spill over. "Whitt, what happens next?" I haven't allowed myself to think of anything beyond being chained to a bed in so long and now that I'm not held down, I don't have a clue what to do.

"Got family, Jess. You get cleaned up, Rebels will be here by then. We'll get you sorted. You have my word."

His eyes meet mine. He doesn't waver. The stare is intense.

"My word, my bond, swear it, Jess, whatever you need, you want, it's a given. Never shoulda let you get caught in this shit. It's on me, not TT. He wanted her in the ground, and I worried what it would do to him inside. I was wrong. He was ready. I was not. You paid the price. I'll spend my every breath to make shit right for you."

The tears spill over in a steady stream. "It's not on you either, Whitton Thorne. Your mom just wasn't right in the head." If I could only be strong enough to tell them, show them, the Thorne twins are not the cause of my pain, their mother did this because she was mentally disturbed.

"You. Have. My. Word. Anything, it's yours." He turns his back to me as his own emotions are at a breaking point. "Swear to fuck, I'll give my life to ease your pain."

"I prayed," I whisper to his back. "I prayed he would never come. I prayed he could find love, have life."

Whitton Thorne turns around to face me. "Too fuckin' good. Damn, Jess, you are too fuckin' good." I can see the glassed over shade in his eyes. "I'm sorry, Jessica. So fuckin' sorry."

"No one touched me, just her." Relief passes in his features. I ramble on. "I could have stayed. Just so that you two could stay out of the mess, I would have kept at it. I could have made it another two years to know that Waylon and you weren't near her. She had venom in her veins toward you, Whitton. She wanted to kill you. No one should live with their mother like that."

For the first time ever, I watch the man in front of me break. Whitton Thorne, all six feet and some inches of him drops to his knees in front of me.

"Whatever God there may be has given you more strength than anyone, more heart than is imaginable, and I swear it, Jess, swear it on my love for Roe, love for the life I got, whatever you want, it's yours."

I drop to my knees in front of him and wrap him gently in my own embrace. With tears dropping onto his head, I hold him close like the broken boy he once was.

"What I want, Whitton Thorne, is to be free. I want to know Waylon can find his peace, you find yours, and in that I will find my own. What I want, Whitton Thorne, is for you to let go of the scars, live your life."

There is a knock at the door, and I jump. Whitton stands leaving me empty on the floor. He pulls a gun from his back just as a man speaks on the other side. "Skinny, open up."

He looks at me. "Go shower, gotta talk to the boys. You're safe, Jess. Every Rebel will lay down their life before anyone gets to you again."

I bite my bottom lip wishing Waylon was here.

"On. My. Word."

With that, I nod and turn around to go shower. Behind the door, I stare blankly at the shower like something might jump out and grab me.

"Shamus, brother, gotta get to TT. Need a clean up," I hear Whitton talk in the other room.

"Got men on it, but you look like hell. We need to get you checked, brother," the other man says.

"Got hit by a car." I hear a thud, and my shower is immediately forgotten as I rush out from the bathroom to find Whitton unconscious on the floor and the other man with short spikey hair standing over him. I see tattoos peek out on his shoulder from under his t-shirt and leather vest covered in patches.

He ignores me completely while yanking out a phone and calling for help. I move to Whitton's side.

"No fuckin' dying on me, Whitton Thorne!" I yell at him, not concerned with my lack of clothing. There is a stranger here, and I sit in panties and a t-shirt hoping Whitton will be okay.

The other man rests a hand on my shoulder, and I jump at the contact.

"Whoa, whoa, name's Shamus." He flicks a hand in front of my face with a tattooed ring finger. "Got a woman, got a kid, not gonna hurt you. Give you my word."

Immediately, my attention goes back to Whitton. "Dammit, you gave me your word! Whatever I wanted. Well, I want you to wake up, be okay, and I wanna see Roe." The words tumble out as the panic rises. I don't know where Waylon is, if he's okay, and now Whitton has obviously been shot, hit by a car, and still came to save me.

He can't die. Not here in front of me. I can't have that on my conscious.

Everything happened at the house so fast, I can't help but worry now if Waylon is okay. He was shot. He had a bleeding wound. Is he on the floor alone?

I feel dizzy as it all consumes me.

The last thing I ever want is for Waylon to be alone.

Shamus yells out the door, and several guys come charging in. I rise on shaky legs and move back, but fall on my ass in the process. An older man with a short trimmed beard, brown eyes, and tattoos that go all the way up his neck blending into his beard, comes toward me and kneels in front of me.

"I'm Lurch. I'm a brother in the Rebels and we're not gonna hurt you, but we need to work on Skinny and get him goin'. Don't be scared, but we're gonna be movin' around a bit."

I nod as the man doesn't touch me, gets up and moves over to Whitton who has a guy with paddles shocking him. His body jolts and mine follows suit.

Moments, that feel like hours later, Whitton groans, "Fuck that hurt."

"Need to get the bullet out and find out what damage there is," another man says, pulling out scissors and cutting away parts of Whitton's clothes. Then as if it's a normal every day thing, he pulls out a scalpel and cuts into Whitton's flesh. He barks out in pain then clamps it down.

Another man hands him a bottle of whiskey, and he pours it inside the wound. Whitton yells again, and

Shamus pulls off his belt and sets it between Whitton's teeth.

Strange, but I guess if it stops him from screaming so be it.

Whitton looks over at me. "I'm good, Jessica. A little stitch up and I'll be back to new." He turns his head. "Shamus, grab my bag or TT's, whichever you find, and grab Jessica some clothes." Shamus nods and leaves. He turns back to me wincing. "Want you to take a shower and get that woman off of you and change into the clothes. Do that for me?" I can see the pain in his eyes, but he's trying to hold it together all to get me to take a shower.

"Get her off you, Jessica, please."

I look around the room at all the strange men and the last thing I really want to do is get naked and shower. He seems to sense my fears.

"Lock the door, Jessica, and no one will go in there. Swear it."

Shamus enters again handing me some clothes and his hand. Shakily, I take it and he helps me to my feet. "Go on in and get cleaned up."

I only nod, go into the bathroom and lock the door. Only then do I put my back to the wood and slide down it, my ass resting on the floor. Tears for the last two missed years spill everywhere and even ones for Waylon.

Being in his arms, I felt safe for the first time in years. Then he tossed me to his brother. It hurts. His brother has a life. Whitton has this love, this passion, and he might lose it all because they came to save me.

**

After picking myself up off the floor, showering and standing under the hot spray until the water changed to cold, I got out, changed, and that leaves me to now. I stare in the mirror and the reflection back at me is one I remember. It's of a woman who has been broken for so long I'm not sure where to find the pieces to rebuild.

My face is so sunken in; I don't resemble the woman I once was. Instead, a malnourished person whose eyes are almost too big for their head stares back at me. No wonder Waylon ran for the hills. I would have to if I'd seen this.

I comb my hair with my fingers, a task I'm used to, and pieces of it break off and flutter to the ground.

It feels so damn good to stand that I bend my knees over and over again getting the feeling back everywhere.

Sucking in a deep breath, I open the door. Whitton is laying on the bed, bandages surrounding his shoulder. Shamus and Lurch sit on the bed by him, and he tries to lift his head to me but lets it fall back down to the pillow.

"Come on out here, Jessica," he calls, and I slowly make my way over there.

"How are you?"

"Patched up and ready to ride another day."

While he did look patched up, I didn't think riding would be on his agenda for a while; more like bedrest.

A motorcycle goes off in the parking look. "Fuck, that's my bike!" Whitton cries out when he moves sitting up and going to the window. “Fuckin’ TT is takin’ my bike. I’m gonna beat his ass.”

I follow Whitton to the window and only get a glace of Waylon from the back, and then he’s gone.

“Find out where the fuck he’s goin’.” This came from Lurch, and Shamus got on his phone and started talking to someone.

Whitton comes over to me, anger gone, but concern there. “I want you to come to the Rebels with me. Roe will love to see ya, and you need some time to get back on your feet. It’ll be a place where we can keep you safe.”

“Safe from what?”

“That, I don’t know, but safe from life, at this point, and I think you need that.”

I nod and having nowhere else to go and no one else to count on, I guess it’s my best option to go back to the Rebels with him.

CHAPTER 12

THERE IS NO SOOTHING MY SOUL, NOT EVEN THE OPEN FUCKIN' ROAD!

TRIPLE THREAT

Twisting the throttle, I press on. Whitton, no doubt, wants to beat my ass for taking his bike. He'll get the fuck over it. I can't see her. I can't look at her and know she's endured two years of some fucked up hell because she tied herself to me.

I knew better then, and I know better now.

No entanglements.

The phone call plays on and on in my mind. Some sick fuck knew about me, knew about Jessica. Even with my cunt mother dead, Jessica isn't safe.

My brain battles a war with my heart. I need to stay away from her, far fucking away, but I may be the only one who can protect her. When did things change? Who did my mother align herself with? The memories seem to shift as I think back.

"Waylon, sweet boy"—her voice is soft, not the high-pitched screech she gives to Whitton—

"you never cry. It's a sign of your strength. He chose you."

I don't know how old I was but I can remember Whitton, just a little before bed, crying out in pain as she bathed him. As we dressed for bed, his skin was red, raw, and scalded. She never did any of this to me.

Always Whitton. Time after time, it was him. She always said he chose me. We always assumed she meant God. Maybe he is a real person.

Needing the support of the club, I take the next exit and head home. Loose gravel gets under the back tire at the exit, and I fight to steady the machine under me. It's not my bagger. My Harley Davidson Street Glide was custom stretched for me when I bought her last year. I have a single seat and no sissy bar because there has never been a bitch to hold onto me. Being on Skinny's ride, feeling that empty space behind me that's reserved for Roe, I can't help but remember that feeling. The one where a single touch makes everything wrong seem okay. I had that with Jessica. I let myself feel. That's my critical mistake. I can only hope Whitton has handled Jessica and set her up somewhere safe.

Somewhere she won't be touched by me and my baggage ever again.

I need a lock on this guy, find out who he is and what he's about. Then take his ass out. No one. And I mean no one is going to hurt Jessica one more second of her life. I've already caused enough hurt for her, and it's my vow that I make her safe. My word, my creed, she'll be free to find love, happiness, and put everything bad behind her.

Jessica always saw the good in me, always thought of me more than I am or was. It turns out she was terribly wrong in her assumptions of me, and I was always right.

She told me once of her dreams for us, owning a house and living together happily. She even talked about renovating it ourselves. Something about making broken beautiful again, turning something out of nothing. I always wondered if that's how she saw me. I was the nothing and she wanted to make something out of me. It was my own twisted way to look at things, but I still can't help it because there is no reason a woman like her should want to be associated with a man like me.

I knew it then, but in my gut—I wanted it. The thought of waking up to her every single morning, getting to kiss her plump lips and come home to her every night was something I craved. It was also something I could never have. When you're born into the shit I was born into, you just know nothing good is ever meant for you.

I knew better. God, I fucking knew better. My mother was wrong, Whitton was the good and I was tainted in evil. Everything I've ever touched from even before my birth has been damaged—

including the woman I love.

Look what's happened to her. Look at the damage I've caused her that she will probably never come back from. All because she loved me. And I loved her.

I will protect her. It's my mission in life to make hers good, by any means necessary.

Several hours later, I pull into the compound and an instant feeling of home comes over me. The peace I was seeking on the open road I couldn't find, yet the instant I find myself here with my brothers I am no longer at war with myself.

Home again.

I'd never had a real one except with the Brown family. The Rebels gave me that. Still give me that. I couldn't accept what the Browns' gave me, didn't know how to process that shit. I'm grown now, and I know what home and peace is. And it's right here.

I may never have love, happiness, and a traditional family, but I have this.

Thumper, Lurch, DJ and Shamus' bikes are in the lot parked. I pull Skinny's bike beside them, cut the engine, and swing my leg off. Skinny comes charging out of the clubhouse, face furious and eyes stabbing me.

"What the fuck!" he barks, getting in my face. "Swear to fuck you were anyone else, I'd fucking gut you right here!" His fists ball up, but he doesn't raise his hand to hit me. I wait for it. I'll take it. "Dammit, TT, you fuckin', you just fucking …" He throws his hands up in the air. "You leave? Just fucking leave?" He points to the clubhouse. "That woman in there needs you. She doesn't need me, brother. She needs you! Where the hell have you been?"

"Ridin'."

"Ridin'." His eye behind the scars on the side of his face twitches, something he only does when he's close to losing control. "If you were any other fuck, takin' off on my bike would get you fuckin' cut, stabbed, the shit beat out of, or a baseball bat to your fucking bike."

"Skinny," I warn, growing tired of the threats. "You wanna beat my ass, here I stand. I'll not take one shot back."

Eye to eye, my twin doesn't stand down, but he doesn't make a move at me either.

"Fucking tough as nails. Genius. You got the IQ of a damn genius. You really think it's smart goin' off alone? Come on, brother! You got me tied in knots and Roe, she's a fuckin' mess worried."

He doesn't mention Jessica, and I'm thankful. I blow out a breath trying to give him the words he needs to calm his shit. "Stopped a couple of times and slept, but needed some time to think."

"You done thinkin' yet?" He blows out a deep breath, steps back, and runs his fingers through his hair. The tension between us leaves.

"No," I tell him the truth. I don't know what's up, down, left, or right. My mother is dead. I should feel like I have all the answers, all the calm, and yet inside I'm still tied up in the chaos of my own making.

He glares at me. "I get you think this shit is your fault. But it's not! That bitch was nuts. We've known it our whole lives." I see his pain. He feels my pain.

"She took Jessica because she thought it would bring me home. Had I known she had her, I would have gone, no questions asked. But instead, Jessica had to live in that hell. How would you feel if Roe lived like that? Huh!?!"

Direct blow.

He physically steps back at my words.

Watching me, he softens in front of me. I see the dread, the fear, and the uncertainty before he speaks. "What if I told you shit ain't over?"

My brother, the man who, since birth, has endured physical pain beyond what the average person can imagine, blinks and I see the fear.

"Too much shit to lose now, Waylon." He drops his head as the weight of my words sink in.

"Bitch got a call while I was at the house. A man. A man who knew me"—he raises an eyebrow at me—"knew Jess."

"Means he knows Roe, too."

I nod. "I don't see how he couldn't."

"Need to get you checked," he says, exhaling deeply. "Shithead, you got shot and took off. Seein' as I had paddles on my chest because the shock of the wreck and the bullet was too much for my ticker, I'm sure you need to get your shit handled sooner rather than later. Infections are a bitch, brother. Let's fix you up and then take this new threat to the table."

"Already told Thumper at the house before clean up."

He moves to stand beside me, with a firm grip on my shoulder, he looks me in the eye. "Glad you're okay, brother. Let's get you checked. The rest of this shit we face together. We sort it, on my word. But fuckin' together, TT!" He looks at me like a father would a son and I nod, giving him the reassurance I won't leave him in the dark again.

Whitton 'Skinny' Thorne is a man of honor, integrity, and heart. There isn't a single doubt in my mind we'll sort this, but it has nothing to do with his word and everything to do with my determination to see Jessica safe.

CHAPTER 13

IS IT POSSIBLE TO BE SCARED OF YOUR SHADOW? YES, YES IT IS!

Jessica

Alabama is beautiful.

Peaceful. Safe. Never thought I'd feel safe in a compound full of bikers, but I do, so much. Roe brought me here after a call from Whitton.

I'm so happy to know they found a way back together. Part of me feels like Whitton left Roe because of me. If Waylon hadn't felt that he was so damaged, he would have stayed with me, and Whitton and Roe wouldn't have lost the time they did.

It's all a tangled mess.

I follow Roe who walks in confidently. Fear immediately consumes me as all these people stand around. Even though they don't seem to give a second notice to me, I haven't been around anyone in so long it panics me.

Sensing this, Roe takes me by the hand, giving me a squeeze, and guides me down a hallway. Whitton comes from a door stopping in front of us. Immediately, he has her wrapped in his arms and his lips pressed to hers.

I've noticed, since we got here, every time he's around her, he has to be touching her, kissing her. It's been so long since I've had normal interaction with people I wonder if this is how a relationship should be. I remember Waylon couldn't keep his hands or eyes off me when we were younger.

It seems like a lifetime ago now.

Following Whitton, we step inside the room he just came from. To the far wall standing in just a pair of jeans is Waylon Thorne. With his back to me, I see his tattoos. A skeleton cloaked in a black robe stands holding a scythe with the words "Triple Threat" on the blade. Above the skeleton is the word ruthless in all caps, old English, and under is the word "rebel", all caps, old English. The eyes of the skeleton are the only thing in color and they are blue, matching Waylon's.

He twists to the side, and my eyes go to his ribs rather than his face. The word "tainted" is in a bold script running up his left side. As I scan upward through the defined muscles of his body, I see his bicep.

There is a life-like heart bleeding with the Hawaiian words, "Kahe mau no kona," bleed for her. Like a magnet finding its other end, I feel pulled to him.

I step to him. He doesn't move. I step closer.

"Waylon," I whisper as my fingers reach out on their own accord to touch his ink.

"Gonna be right outside," Whitton says, but Waylon and I don't move or speak as Whitton and Roe step outside.

"Fuckin' beautiful," he practically growls before turning to face me. His hands grip my neck and tilt my head to look into his eyes. “Love is fuckin’ misery.”

The words hit me the same time his mouth crashes to mine. Stunned, I pause. Opening my mouth to breathe, his tongue invades. Just as I relax and reach out to hold his waist, he pulls back.

“Fuckin’ got no willpower with you,” he pants but doesn’t release me nor do I, him.

“Waylon,” I whisper again as I see his right rib tattooed with the word “lost” in script before noticing the bandage covered spot on his shoulder just above a tattoo of the Hawaiian Islands over his left pectoral muscle.

I’m speechless, breathless, as I fall against him.

His hands slide down my body holding me close.

Home.

Peace.

I can hear the sounds of waves crashing softly on a shore in my mind as my soul finds comfort in this moment. Something I never thought I would get again—ever.

“Wish I could fuckin’ hold you for a lifetime,” I hear him mutter.

I squeeze tighter as he tries to pull away. “Don’t, Waylon. I have nowhere to turn. I don’t know what’s real anymore, please don’t pull away now.”

I feel pathetic to even ask him not to let me go when it’s obvious he wants to, but I lost everything. The one thing I’ve ever wanted for a future is in my arms, and even if I only have it for a moment I want to believe it’s mine.

"Made a call," he rumbles with my head pressed to his chest. His hand strokes my hair while the other holds me close. "Got your pops on a plane. He'll be here tonight."

I swear my heart might leap out of my chest.

My father will be here tonight. I pull back and look Waylon in the eye. "What does he know?"

"Nothin'. Told him you wanted to see him, needed him. What you choose to share is your story to tell, Jessica."

I swallow hard.

"Got you both tickets back to Hawaii in three days. Whitton's got you a new phone but the same number so you can reach your mother. Tried to get word to her, she didn't answer."

My heart shatters all over again.

"She thinks I abandoned my family to live life traveling." Needing space, I step away from him and move to the bed.

He goes to a dresser to pull out a black t-shirt and slide it on. "I'll set her straight, Jess."

"I don't think it's gonna be that easy."

He studies me. "Never said shit would be easy, just said I'll set her straight."

We sit in silence, him staring at me, and me staring at him.

"Wanna ride?" he asks, surprising me.

I bite my bottom lip and nod feeling apprehensive but also like a caged animal needing to feel free.

Taking me by the hand, he leads me back out the way I came in. A man I learned was Shamus, when Whitton was hurt, yells out, "Skinny, better watch out, your brother Triple Threat is gonna give you a run for your money on the caveman life with his woman."

"Shut the fuck up, Shamus. You aren't beyond throwing Andrea over your shoulder to drag her to your lair," Waylon says back, relaxed; surprising me.

This is how bikers joke, interesting. Seeing Waylon here with his family, as both Whitton and he have called them, it's peaceful. I've had so much time away; I feel myself tense in every situation except when I'm around Waylon. Having this time to watch him as a man in his comfort and his place, it's the extra confidence boost I need to remember I'm free of the two years of hell.

I don't have time to think before Waylon has me standing in front of a black motorcycle that is sleek, low to the ground, long, and has these hard sides off the back that stretch out into a tip with chrome peeking out for the exhaust. He leans down and clicks open one of the side pieces which I now see are saddlebags to get a half shell helmet that he promptly hands to me.

Just as I manage to get the buckle secure, he is straddling the beast and has it cranked. The loud engine doesn't rattle me like I thought it would; instead, I find it to be almost rhythmic. He reaches out a hand and looks at me.

"Got no bitch seat or extra pegs, so you gotta hold my hand, swing over and then one leg at a time, I'm gonna wrap you around me."

I do as he says and find myself chest to his back with my legs wrapped around his waist crisscrossed and my arms tight around his chest. The metal of the bags is hard on my ass. My head rests on his shoulder as he rolls us back.

"Never had a woman ride with me like this. Shit feels too good," Waylon mutters more to himself than me. "Dangerous game we're playin' once again."

We take off. The machine comes alive under me. The vibration of the engine goes through me. My body hums feeling alive as the air opens my pores and the sunshine beats down on my exposed skin.

My hair whips around us as I relax more and more into the ride.

Waylon twists the throttle, the engine revs, and we take off faster. Inhaling the hot, humid, Southern air is stifling. The burn reminds me I'm alive.

"I'm alive. I'm free!" I yell out, getting lost in the moment.

Waylon's left hand comes off the handlebar to rest on my inner thigh since I'm sitting indian style around him. The feeling is electric and only surges through my body making me high on life.

We ride for what feels like hours but really was only about an hour before we stop at a small restaurant. Waylon steadies the bike before unpeeling my legs from around him so I can climb off.

On shaking legs, I stand. Waylon drops the kickstand and balances the bike on it before climbing off. He drapes his arm casually over my shoulders and leads us inside. The first few steps feel strange after getting off the bike, but Waylon won't let me fall, I feel it.

**

"WE'RE ON OUR WAY," Waylon says in the phone after picking up my father from the airport. I wanted to go, but with that many people around me, I wasn't sure I could handle it. I've been alone for so long, that being here at the clubhouse is a push.

Waylon saw it and suggested he go and get them. I was grateful for that. He knows me better than most, even after all these years have passed.

Tension builds inside of me. I haven't seen my dad in two years, haven't talked to him in a long time. That woman texted him, but I don't know what she said because she deleted the thread. That woman was deviously smart. I shiver thinking about her then block it out.

Whatever she told my father, I need to deal with. I still don't know if I should tell him everything. Waylon could get in trouble for what he did; that's something I don't want to happen. I also don't want my father to think that I've been having a happy time while we were apart. But if I tell him, he'll worry and now, I'm okay. At least physically. Mentally is a whole other animal.

Time ticks by as I sit on the bed in what I was told was DJ's old room, noting how life still went on even though I wasn't a part of it. The clock still ticked. The sun still went up and down. People in the world kept going, and I felt stuck.

Waylon wants me gone. To live back with my father far away from here—from him. My heart aches, but I refuse to let a tear fall. I've done that enough over the last couple of days.

I don't know where I want to be or where I belong.

A knock comes to the door as Waylon opens it, and I rise from the bed. My father stands there, an unsure look on his face. His dark hair is almost to his shoulders and comes down in waves. His eyebrows are as bushy as usual. Time has been good to him, even as I take in the wrinkles from squinting in the sun or maybe from worry. He's broad shouldered and standing beside Waylon, his five-feet-eight-inch-tall body dwarfs in comparison.

I waste no time and launch myself in his arms wanting to feel his security around me. Security I'd only ever felt with him and Waylon. My father envelops me in his arms and we stand like this for a while, him holding me and me letting him.

My father pulls away and looks at me. I've never been embarrassed by the way I look, but not having the right things to eat and not moving much in the last two years, I know I look bad. My hair lost its vibrancy and will take a while to come back. My skin isn't as plump as it should be, and as he's observing me I feel that insecurity bubble up.

"Dad," I whisper.

"Baby girl. What's going on with you?" Worry lines appear on his forehead, and his brows pull together. The exact thing I didn't want to happen.

"I'm coming home," I announce with a smile on my face that I don't feel one bit. While I love Hawaii, going back right now scares the hell out of me. With my situation, I honestly have nowhere else to go.

He pulls me to the bed, and I sit next to him. "You look sick. Are you sick?"

I shake my head. "No, Dad. Just getting myself back on track." For some reason, I don't tell him. I don't tell him I was captive for two years. I don't tell him what that woman did to me. I don't tell him anything, and I tell myself it's because I'm protecting Waylon. But I'm protecting my father as well.

"You've been traveling, huh?"

"Yeah," I lie and hear a grunt by the door. Waylon's face is pissed. He must have thought I would tell my father, but that's my business. He wants to be mad, that's on him.

Not wanting to answer any questions about *my travels* I ask, "How have you been?"

He smiles wide. "I met someone, we actually got married about a year ago."

Stunned, I ask, "How? Mom said she would never sign papers; she just didn't like island life."

"Your mom has changed. She has hardened herself. She had me served without even a call in warning. I figured it was really done then, so life moves on and so did my heart."

My heart cracks, another thing I missed.

"Congratulations, Dad," I whisper, feeling that grief in the gut.

He reaches out and grabs my hand. "Can't wait for you to meet her." As much as it sounds great, I'm not feeling it at all. Life definitely went on. I don't lead on to that.

"Yeah."

"You say you're coming home. Are you getting a place?"

Fear grips ahold of me. I have no money. I have no possessions. I have nothing but the clothes on my back, and that's because Roe gave them to me. There is no way I can afford my own place.

"I was hoping to stay with you, Dad."

His face changes in a way that doesn't look good for my future. "Stella and I, we don't have any room. We had to downsize."

Gripping my hands together it feels like a large boulder is resting on my chest. Now, I really have nowhere to go.

"Right."

"I mean, you're welcome to visit and sleep on the couch a coupla nights, but to stay with us isn't possible."

"I understand." Technically, as far as he knew, I'd been on my own for years. Before I was taken, I had a job and an apartment. It wasn't the best, but I made due. Now, there was none of that.

"How about we go eat? I'm starved."

My eyes shoot to Waylon as the panic hit of being around people, then I dart them away. He can't protect me. He doesn't want that responsibility, and he shouldn't have it. Somehow, some way, I'm going to have to stand on my own two feet. I just don't know how to do that. I'll damn well figure it out, though.

"Sounds good." He taps my leg and rises from the bed. I follow him to the door.

I look up at Waylon. “Thanks for bringing my dad here.”

“I’m coming,” he declares, and I shake my head.

“No, you’re off duty, Waylon.” My father, now down the hall, clears his throat so I hurry out. “I’ll figure myself out and be out of here.”

He goes to grab my arm, but I pull away and make it to my father. This will be a challenge, but one step at a time. I’ve got to do this.

CHAPTER 14

THERE'S NO SUCH THING AS A CLEAN BREAK WHEN IT'S REAL LOVE!

TRIPLE THREAT

He's not going to let her stay with him, and I'm pissed as hell she didn't tell him what she's gone through the last two years. Her father should know. But it's her decision. I don't have to like it, though. Maybe she will tell him while they eat. They need time to reconnect, and then she needs to share the truth.

This wasn't her fault. She shouldn't suffer more because once upon a time she fell in love with me.

I watch as she leaves with her father, and instinct has me wanting to follow her. She's not ready for crowds. I bite back the urge.

"Where's she goin'?" Skinny asks as I move into the clubhouse main room.

"To get food with him."

"She ready for that?"

"Nope." We take a seat at the bar, and I slap my hand down. A prospect brings me a beer, and I take a large swig. "He's not letting her stay with him, either. And I can't get ahold of her mother. She's bein' a bitch."

"So what do you suggest?"

"Fuck if I know, but she can't stay here." I turn to my brother. "You find anything."

He shakes his head. “Nope. Nothin’. We’re pullin’ in everything to get some crumbs, but whoever this fucker is—he’s smart. The phone number leads to a pre-paid phone that is no longer in service. We’re hopin’ that Logic can use the locator and give us an idea of where this guy is. If he’s back in Ohio where bitch held Jessica or somewhere close.”

Logic is our tech guru with hacker skills that could land the man with a life sentence in maximum security. If he can’t find a trace, then we’re fucked. “She stays here, she’s in danger.”

“She stays here; she’s got you to protect her,” he fires back.

“Like I did from our mother,” I say, standing and walking off leaving my beer and brother behind.

I feel like a caged animal.

Jessica was caged … trapped, tormented mentally, and I still don’t even have the fucking balls to face if there was anything more done to her.

I feel the need to run. Far. Wide. Fast. I need to get away. Her wrapped around me on my bike…

Fucking shit is heaven.

It’s yet another selfish as fuck memory I’ll hold onto until my last damn breath. After this meeting, there is a strong chance Jessica will return to Hawaii with her father. I hope they can find a way to make it work. It’s the best thing she can do for herself.

Years, I’ve had this terrible burn inside for the dark haired beauty currently down the road. I survived, and I will get through this, too.

An hour passes, all the while, I stand outside the clubhouse lost in a way I've never been before.

Drifters.

All our lives, Skinny and I have been on this path going nowhere. Then we found the Rebels. In the club, with the brothers, we found our place. Confidently, we have thrived in life. When all the cards were stacked against us, this club gave us a home.

He found Roe again—love, life, happiness. They have it all. I look at the building; I look at my bike. Our mother is dead. The club will find the fuck behind the call … then what?

Where do I fit in now that my past no longer follows me?

They finally come back, Jessica's eyes are puffy from crying and her dad's show the redness of his own emotions. Involuntarily, as if blinking, I reach out and find myself pulling Jessica into my arms with her back to my chest. I need to stop, but I can't. Every time she's near me, I have to hold her close, touch her, feel her with me.

"Waylon," he says to me, and I nod. "A word?" Studying the man and watching Jessica's eyes grow wide, I see she's shared at least some of what she's gone through with her father. The man possibly, and rightfully so, wants to kill me.

With a kiss to the top of her head, I step away immediately feeling the loss of her. Whitton, DJ, and Shamus step outside giving me a calm in knowing she will have some protection since we're still trying to sort out the man on the phone and the danger level.

Lurch shadowed them at their meal but needed to get home for the day.

"Chill with Skinny for a few," I tell her before stepping to the side of the building with her father.

I follow the man who is nowhere near my height or build to a set of tables away from the bar and noise.

"Just gonna cut to the chase here, I wanna kill you for the pain she's endured, the pain I have endured. I understand your mother was a sick woman. I understand she is no longer a threat, and I can use my imagination on how Jessica can be so sure of this. I have just one daughter, Waylon. She is my light, my love for her is larger than the ocean is big."

Guilt eats at me as the man speaks. For the first time in my life, I find myself too ashamed to meet a man's eyes.

"She still loves you. Even after all this, she has no hatred for you. That's a connection in my culture, of destiny. For that, I will allow her to stay here as she has asked and, honestly, I don't have the space or resources to bring her home. I would do anything if it's where she wanted to be, but it's not. She is tied to you and feels it."

"She's better off with you," I reply. knowing it's the truth.

The man doesn't cower from my stare. "She's dead inside if she leaves you, as are you if she were to go."

I lift my head to meet his brown eyes. "Better than the not breathin' kind of dead she can land herself tied to me."

Before he can say another word, before I can let the truth behind my words sink in, I turn and walk away.

Reaching my bike, I don't look at her. I don't look at my club brothers or my twin brother. Instead, I put my bike in gear, roll backward, and then back in gear, crank the beast, and take off. If I dared glance up to find her watching me, I would know without a doubt that what her father says is the truth.

Tormented.

Plagued.

Pained.

The road passes under me, inch after inch, mile after mile, my chest burns.

The agony is relentless.

The wind hits my face. I press on. I ride and ride. The further I go; the more pain I feel course through my body. Pulling over on a dirt road, I follow it through a wooded area to a clearing.

The craftsman house in front of me has seen better days. The shudders are missing, and the windows are either broken or open like they are stuck. Layers of worn paint show, and the front steps are missing railings.

I park.

In my mind, I can see this house redone in grays and navy blues. The shed in the back that is leaning precariously to the right can easily be expanded to house a car and tools.

Climbing off my bike, I walk up to the front door. Turning the knob, the door pops open. Hardwood floors cover the inside. They look solid just covered in dust. The walls are sheetrock that although in need of a fresh coat of paint, everything looks structurally sound.

Lifting my phone, I make the call.

"Lo," Thumper answers.

"An hour past Old Mill Road, the dirt road, there's a house, I need to buy it."

I hear him give a soft chuckle in the phone. This is no laughing matter. "My boys are growing up. We'll sort out who owns it and get it covered."

"No matter the cost. All cash. Close in three days," I clip out, knowing that if anyone can make shit happen it's Thumper.

"Consider it done."

At his words, all the tension leaves my body. Destiny.

This feels right.

I head back to my bike and back to Jessica.

Skinny stands out front waiting on me, no doubt in my mind he would rather be home with Roe, but he wants to kick my ass first.

"Where is she?" I ask rather than greet him.

"Roe took her and her dad back to the house since we weren't sure if you could pull your head outta your ass."

Before I can reply, Thumper comes out with a thick envelope in hand.

"Goin' to pick up your keys," he says to me and gives Skinny a nod.

"That easy?"

"Know a guy who knows the family that inherited the house. Shit's been empty for three years. Needs clean up, but they wanna sell. I said all cash and offered ten grand over the asking price last time they had it on the market if I could pick up keys today."

"Shit," I tell him, stunned and relieved.

"Gotta head to the lawyer's office to drop the cash off so she can handle the papers. They're leaving the keys there and said we could start tonight. Got ten days tied up for the paperwork, but the house is yours."

"Hers," I correct. "It goes in Jessica's name. Clean it up enough for her to live there, but she always wanted to have a fixer upper. House goes in her name; I'll cover the bills."

Thumper nods before climbing on his bike to take care of buying Jessica a house. Her dad can't take her in. Skinny says she's not safe away from here, so problem solved. She can have her life back, and I can know she's okay when I leave.

"Why do I get the feeling your ass doesn't plan on bein' in that house with her?"

"She needs a place to stay. I'm facilitatin' it."

He drops his head to look at the ground before lifting it and looking me in the eyes. "She needs to be safe. She needs to remember what it is to be free. She needs to have a family. Way I see it, she can get all that right here with you."

"Skinny, don't push. I'm doing the best I can. I cost her enough, I won't fuck up her future."

"Mom's in the ground. Nothing left to fuck shit up anymore but you."

Without giving me a chance to respond, he walks to his bike.

“Way I see it, God, destiny, fate, fuckin’ Aphrodite, decidin’ you should have a second chance at love.” I shake my head as he cranks his bike. “Question you gotta ask yourself, brother, you man enough to take it?”

CHAPTER 15

WHEN YOU HAVE NO WHERE TO GO BUT IT'S STILL BETTER THAN WHERE YOU'VE BEEN – THAT'S A WIN RIGHT?

Jessica

"You're staying with us," Roe declares, moving around the kitchen putting fruit in a bowl. Upon asking her to help, she said no. Instead, I sit at the kitchen table with my father next to me watching me like a hawk. Which I can't blame him. I did drop a bomb on him at dinner.

I hadn't planned to share. He just kept looking at me with his chocolate brown eyes that were my safe place as a child, and I couldn't let him think I had purposely missed life. Then the thoughts of him leaving with questions unanswered … I couldn't do it.

I couldn't let him go home without him knowing why I stayed away for so long. Why I missed so many things in his life. He deserved to know, and it killed me telling him.

He has a life, though, and I don't fit in that. Therefore, I told him I'd stay here, not having the slightest clue where or how I'd make that work. It gave him an out, and that's what he needed.

"Roe, that's really nice, but I don't know…if this is where I should be." Not that I have many choices, but staying with Waylon's brother and woman doesn't seem like the best idea. Especially when Waylon can't even look at me. I noticed. Like some lovesick fool, I watched, waited for him to look at me. It didn't happen. He wants nothing to do with me. Not going to lie, that kills deep inside me.

My father kept talking to me through dinner about destiny and how Waylon and I got a second chance at life. My father is normally right about these things, but in this case, I have to differ.

Destiny isn't for everyone. Mine was carved out a while ago by a crazy woman. Now, I don't believe that's an option for me. In fact, I don't know that I believe in much anymore.

"Nonsense. You're staying here. We have an extra room, and you need to get back on your feet." Roe comes to the table with the bowl, sets it down, and scoops a little in a smaller bowl already on the table. Then she begins to eat all the while motioning us to eat.

"I'm not hungry." It's not a lie. I haven't eaten much in a long time so big meals are difficult, but smaller portions, regularly, I find myself always hungry.

Roe looks at me, her eyes worrisome. She looks at my father, almost as if she's begging me to tell him everything will be okay. I, too, see the concern in his features, but I can't tell him anything will be alright when I, myself, don't believe it.

"You want to tell me what's going on with Waylon?" my father asks, studying me like a science experiment about to go wrong.

I shrug. "He has some things he's working through."

Roe scoffs, "No, he feels guilty for what happened to Jessica." She looks to me. "Jessica, we used to be friends, and I know the past. I also know Waylon. It's riding on him hard, and he doesn't know how to fix it." She looks back at my father. "Waylon's a man who takes care of his family and knowing Jessica was going through that and he wasn't there to stop it, is riding on him hard." She turns back to me and rests her hand on mine. "He has a soft heart. Under all that hard shell, he cares and does it with everything he has. Give him some time."

"Time seems to be all I have right now."

She gives me a smile. "Yes, time to get yourself sorted. Here, with us."

"Only for a while," I finally concede. This is temporary until I can figure something else out.

Time flies talking to Roe and Dad, but in the back of my mind, I worry about where Waylon is. If he's okay and if he'll come and find me. I shouldn't, but I can't help it.

Before I know it, it's night then the next morning and my father leaves to go back to Hawaii. Saying goodbye is never easy, but he has a life to get back to.

One that went on without me.

Two days later

No Waylon. Not a single word, and I didn't dare ask Whitton anything about him. He's obviously done with me, and it's time for me to get my life back. I could wallow and let what happened to me change me forever. I could easily crawl into myself and hide out there, but I refuse. I spent enough time stuck with me, myself, and I.

Time to get back up and kick the dust off.

I'm scared, but I won't let this define me.

What happened, sucks. I don't wish it upon anyone, but it will not define me as a person. I will not look back and say Jessica Quemuel was kidnapped and held captive. No. That is not how I will be remembered.

Roe has given me some clothes so at least I have that. Small steps, but I will get me back. We are going to the bank later to see if my account is still active. I had a little saved before, but I don't know if MaryRuth took it or not.

My phone rings, my first thought being *it's Waylon.* I dart to it and note it's a number I don't know. I answer.

"My sweet Jessica. So lovely to hear your voice," a strange male voice says over the phone line.

"Who is this?"

"I just knew you'd bring our Waylon back to us," he says instead of answering my question. "He's always loved you." His words are a stab to the heart, but I say nothing about that.

"Who is this and what do you want?"

The man gives a chuckle. "I want Waylon, of course, and you're going to help me get him."

"What do you mean *get him?* He's not an object." My voice hitches. This is hell. A mindfuck. She always wanted to get him, like he was a possession.

"Such fire. MaryRuth always underestimated people, but not me. I knew underneath you had a spark. One our Waylon couldn't resist. She should have reached out before and pulled him in. I told her, but she always said her mother's bond was strong and he would find the two of you. It was my lesson in patience, I suppose."

Whoever this man is, he's as nuts as Waylon's mother. "I'm not helping you do anything. Don't call me back."

"Don't hang up or I'll kill Waylon, Whitton, and that beautiful Roelyn Duprey."

My heart stops and breaths become hard to take in.

"Judging by your silence I got your attention." He gives a soft chuckle. "You bring him to me."

"I'm not going to bring him to you so you can kill him!" I shriek a little loudly.

I may have been held against my will for a long time, but that doesn't mean I'm stupid as hell. No way I'd lead Waylon to be killed by anyone. Especially whoever the hell this is on the phone.

"Heard your father was in town and went back to Hawaii. It'd be a shame if something was to happen to him. He is so in love with his wife. Your mother, well, she isn't hard to find either. In fact, I could give you her exact location right this minute. It's a shame she won't take your calls," he says, his voice going low. "Collateral damage."

Acid turns in my stomach threatening to come up.

"Stay away from my father, me, and Waylon! Everyone!" My body begins to shake just as the door to my room opens and Whitton is standing there, his eyes narrow. Tears spring to mine, rapidly falling down my face.

"You bring him to me, and you'll save him," the man says.

"Save him from who?" I bite back, wanting to know who's on the other end of the phone. Needing to know who has rained down this hell on us all.

Whitton takes the phone from my ear. "Who the fuck is this?" Whitton pulls the phone from his ear. "Fuck, they hung up." He looks at me. "Who was it? What did they want?"

"I don't know. Some man. He threatened to kill Waylon and my father," I hiccup. "You, Roe, my mother. He is going to take everyone if I don't bring Waylon to him. I don't know who he is." Sobs escape me.

"Fuck!" he growls and pulls out his phone punching in some numbers, then holding it up to his ear. "Get your fuckin' ass to my house now." He clicks off the phone then does this a couple more times before he leaves the room taking my phone with him.

Deep in my gut, I know this is bad. Really bad.

Standing alone in the room, knowing the danger surrounds everyone I care for, fear grips me. I close my eyes and take a deep breath. Clasping my hands together, I raise them to my chin, bow my head, and do something I don't even know if it's real … I pray.

I'm down to nothing. There's not a single thing I can do to save myself or anyone around me.

For the first time, I feel defeated. There is no acceptance of my situation. There is no escape for any of us.

We're all doomed to a hell unlike no other. It is what it fucking is. I give up.

CHAPTER 16

SHE OWNED ME BEFORE I EVER MADE MY CLAIM!

TRIPLE THREAT

I pull up to Skinny's house right behind Lurch, DJ, and Shamus. Well, the gang's all here—I knew shit was bad by my brother's tone, for him to call everyone—shit's out of control.

I don't go inside.

The pull to go to her, to place my lips to hers, and hold her is growing stronger.

I am stronger.

I fucked this shit up for her. I won't drag her down more.

Skinny storms out of his front door, knife on his side, Glock in a shoulder strap. His eyes scream evil.

He stomps straight to me. I sit on my bike as he grabs the edges of my cut and yanks me up.

I allow the move.

"Fucking called her! I got your woman in my house, tears flowing, and a twat-lovin-sick-fuck threatening her to the point of tears." I stand face to face with him. "Tears for you!"

He doesn't hit me, but his words are an assault all their own.

"Fuckin' locked up, starved, degraded, and we'll never know what else and she's in my house sheddin' fuckin' tears tryin' to protect your ass."

DJ comes to stand beside me. "Skinny, Thumper got a lead off the phone. We're gonna get him. She's safe. Let TT off the hook, brother."

The anger pulses so fiercely through my twin, I can see the vein in his neck throbbing. "Too fuckin' smart for this shit. Your ass needs to be schooled in something more than vengeance and withdrawal. Stayin' away from her didn't do shit for either of you. Got her inside with tears! Tears, asshole."

"Back off, Skinny." DJ steps up to my twin trying to take my back.

"No," I say to DJ, but never waver from my brother's stare. "I'm never off the hook."

"You're not, I'm not, but you're who she wants and who she needs, so go give her that before we go make this shit right with the sick fuck on the phone."

DJ and Shamus seem lost, but I know what Skinny wants me to do.

He's right.

I don't speak, I make my way inside the house.

Going straight to Jessica's room, I pass Roe at a quick clip. Opening the door, I find Jessica laying on the bed curled in a ball with tears falling onto the pillow under her. I will never forget the pain in her eyes when they meet mine. Rushing to her, I drop to my knees beside the bed as she sits up. Gripping her hips, I lean up and press my lips to her cheek.

The salt of her tears hits my lips before I pull back and whisper, "Gonna make shit right."

"He's gonna kill you," she replies with a broken voice.

"No, he's not. On my word, Jess, swear to fuck, I'm gonna make shit right. You are mine. This shit between us, no amount of time has changed. Fuckin' loved you then, love you now. Not gonna run, not gonna hide, and not gonna let one bad thing touch you again for the rest of my fuckin' life, baby."

She sobs. "Waylon, he wants you. I prayed to whoever that you would never find me. I'd go back to that bed if it meant you were safe."

"It's my job, as your man, to protect you. Not yours to protect me. I'm gonna make you safe. I'm gonna make shit safe. No more sacrificing yourself for me. Baby, I'm shit and don't deserve that love, that loyalty."

Her hands shake as she cups my face and moves to rest her forehead to mine. "What are we gonna do? He wants you."

"He doesn't get me. You got me. You stay with Roelyn. When I get back, I got us a place. I don't know how shit will go, but from this moment on we do it together."

She hiccups back the emotions before taking a deep breath. "Peace," she whispers. "You give me peace in the worst of storms."

"You give me peace always, baby. No matter the time, the distance, or the situation, you've always been my calm in the chaos, Jessica."

The rumble of more bikes pulling up can be heard outside. I press my lips to hers. Willingly she opens herself to me, and I take.

I claim.

From this second on, she is mine. I will take out any fucker who poses a threat to her, me, or the future we're going to have.

Our lips battle and our tongues tangle as my emotions stop the crazy war we've been on. I pull her off the bed, onto my lap, and she straddles me as I sit on my knees pinning her between my body and the bed. Jessica is mine.

Mine to protect.

Mine to love.

Pulling away, I see her eyes are glazed over in a fog of her own emotions.

"Waylon, please don't go."

Gliding my hands up her body, I cup her face tenderly. "Promise you, I'll be back. Promise you, when I come back, nothing from the past will be between us again."

"I'm worried about you, about Whitton, about us all."

"Got people at my back, baby. Got family. Whit and I need to handle this shit for you, for Roe, for all of us."

Slowly, we break apart and she stands. I stand pulling her to me. Her head hits my chest and I inhale.

A calm washes over me.

A calm in a storm that is raging on.

A calm I refuse to ever lose again.

"Sit tight with Roe. Don't know how long we'll be, but you'll be safe here, promise."

She turns and lifts her head to look up at me. Immediately, I drop my lips to hers again.

She squeezes me tightly before I hear Whitton yelling my name from the door.

"Gotta go."

We separate, and I see her blow out a breath to gather strength. "E pakele, be safe."

"Always."

Destiny. Fate. Fucking Aphrodite. I don't give a shit who gave me this second chance, but I won't fuck it up.

Making my way out of her room and down the hall, my twin meets my stare, searching. "All is well," I say, giving him the confirmation he's seeking.

"We got an hour ride, plans bein' made outside. Got eyes on the house so Roe and Jess are safe."

I nod.

He moves past me to find Roe and kisses her hard.

"Love you," he tells her, to which she smiles at him.

Yes, today we leave any danger from the past behind us. For Roe, for Whitton, for Jessica, and for me.

Born to shit doesn't mean we have to live in shit.

The hour drive feels like three as I follow Lurch and Thumper into a park off the beaten path. The bikes cut, and we climb off moving into a circle and stretching our legs. Thumper is looking at his phone, tapping things in. DJ is doing the same, but he has a wicked smile.

"Need the info," I say when no one says anything right away. "Need this shit done." Skinny comes to stand beside me, having my back just as I have his. Brothers by blood and choice.

"Do you know a man named Gerald Walker?"

"Fuck no," I answer as Skinny shakes his head.

"The trace came back to him. Lives in a quaint house about a mile from here and our destination."

"What do ya have on him?" I ask.

Thumper shakes his head. "Not much. I've got the location and people on it, but nothing yet."

"So, we're goin' in blind," Skinny says next to me.

"You wanted me schooled in love; well, this fucker needs to be schooled in fuckin' with family. Don't give a fuck we gotta do it blind with our hands behind our back. This fucker is done. He's threatened those we love, and you don't threaten a Rebel."

"Head out. We'll park a block out and head up on foot. Even if he has a security system, the chances of him wanting the cops involved are slim. Think of him as armed and ready."

We pull out and move quickly a block away, then get off and take the rest on foot, but keep separated enough that we aren't noticed.

I make it up to the address and stop dead.

"You've got to be shittin' me," Skinny clips out as we both stare at a church. Several peaks and valleys throughout the tanned structure with large crosses on three different places including the top. The large parking lot is empty, but that doesn't mean there aren't eyes. Church people have a thing about protecting their own, at least that's what's been instilled in Skinny and me over our childhood.

Off to the side is a house that is connected to the church.

"Fuck, is he a pastor?"

Skinny shrugs. "Doesn't fuckin' matter. His God can't save him now."

Thumper nods his head to the small house, and I take off. Twisting the handle on the door, it opens immediately as I step through with my gun in hand at the ready.

"My son has finally arrived!" A man I've never seen before steps into the room, his hands raised above his head like he's absorbing some kind of power above him. His short gray hair is balding on the top, and his mustache is curved at the tips. He has on plain clothes, jeans and a t-shirt.

"You called?" I ask, my gun pointed at the man as I feel Skinny approach from behind.

The man's face changes. "You brought him!" he yells, anger marring his face now. "Devil! The evil must be gone!" He looks at me in fury. "We must cleanse you, my son. He is all things bad. The prophecy was shown. Whitton is the Devil cometh again."

Skinny holds up his gun. "Fuck yeah, and I'm happy to be your executioner."

"Should have known the Devil would never let you go! You're a disgrace and no son of mine!" the asshole yells and considering we're standing in the same fucking room is annoying as hell.

"Sure as shit no son of yours."

A sinister smile comes across Gerald's face. "We may share the same DNA, Waylon and me, but the Devil spouted you, Whitton!"

"Blah blah blah. That bitch warped you, too." Skinny's easy demeanor is only a front for what's about to come for this man. Me, I'm stuck on the sharing the same DNA shit he just said.

"What do you mean, share the same DNA?" I ask as Skinny tilts his head, and I feel more Rebels enter the room.

"What is this, a fuckin' party?" Shamus says, moving to my left while DJ moves to Skinny's right. "Church ain't my thing, but I'm sure we'll make this shit fun, too."

"Answer!" I bark at Gerald, but his eyes stay on the men around us.

"You are my son. I impregnated your mother solely for you to be born. God told me too, said you'd bring life back to our world. Make it a better place. That you would clean up all the bad and keep the good. The Devil attacked her while she was pregnant, though, and gave us him," he growls at my brother.

I should feel something, but I don't. This man is nothing to me. Will never be anything to me.

"You're old enough to be my grandpa," Skinny says on a chuckle. "I mean, robbin' the cradle?"

Gerald's face turns fierce. "MaryRuth had potential. I was her youth minister, you Devil! God told me it was her. Told me what I needed to do. I have no regrets." He reaches behind his back and pulls out a gun aiming it at Skinny. "He has to die!"

I aim and fire, dropping the man to the ground, just as he shoots his gun. Luckily, the man has horrible aim and hits the drywall behind Skinny. Walking closer, Gerald coughs, having dropped the gun to the floor, I kick it to the side.

"What you need to know is—I'm the Devil. I'm the one you need to watch out for. When you meet whatever God you think you know, you'll never find peace. Rest assured—I will." His eyes widen as I aim at his forehead and shoot, no hesitation, no question. He's a threat that needs to be extinguished. Now, there is no more.

"I'll call clean up. Fuck, can't believe this is a church. Could be tricky people, even gangsters have their morals, ya know," Thumper says, pulling out his phone then looking at me. "He's no father. You know better than most—DNA means shit when it comes to family."

He's right, and I wouldn't have it any other way.

My family has my back right here, right now. My family is my future and what the fuck I make it.

CHAPTER 17

MINE! FOUR LETTERS WITH WEIGHT, MEANING, AND EMOTION THAT FILL ME BEYOND FULL!

Jessica

One week later

THE BED SHIFTS and I jolt awake trying to sit up, but a steel arm is around my middle. "Got ya," Waylon says and I calm, instantly falling back to the bed. He curls his body against mine, the heat taking care of my chilled body. He's been my source of strength and my comfort when the nightmares come.

"Are you okay?" I whisper into the room.

His arms tighten. "Now, yeah."

"I've missed you."

"Only been gone a few hours, baby."

I reach out and tap his leg. "You know what I mean." He has only been gone a few hours, working. I don't know what that means, but I've learned when he works it's for the Rebels. Roe says don't ask about the club. Part of me is curious, but after having two years of my life stripped from me, I'm happy to simply be in the moment.

He chuckles, a sound I never thought I'd hear again. A sound that kept me warm on the cold nights.

"Missed you too, Jess. Every fuckin' day."

It's hard to believe with everything between us that in this moment I feel full, complete. I don't know what it is about Waylon Thorne, or what we share that is able to soothe every fear I have. Our love knows no boundaries, no distance, and no time. He is everything I've ever needed, wanted, and craved.

I roll in his arms to look in his eyes. "Don't leave me again, Waylon."

He leans down and kisses my lips. "Never. Till death do us part, Jess. From now until forever."

Attaching my lips to mine, I kiss him with everything I have inside of me. All the fear, all the love, all that is me. He reciprocates pulling me tight to his body, our legs intertwining. He has no pants on, just his boxers, and the skin to skin contact is amazing.

His rough hands move up my back, one resting on the nape of my neck. His lips caress mine as his tongue sweeps inside my mouth. The taste that is all Waylon overcomes me, and I feel lost. Lost in him. Lost in the moment. Lost in us.

Waylon takes his time with my lips, and my hands roam his hard body. He's not the boy he was before. Life has given him experience which I flip off in my head, because I don't need to have it.

He kisses down my neck, pulls off my shirt, my back arching. His kisses continue all down my body and my core clenches, my panties becoming damp. It's been so long. So long, I forgot what this feels like.

What it means to be aroused.

What it means to want a man.

To want Waylon.

My panties are torn from my body, and I'm pushed to my back. Waylon's head dips down, and my back leaves the bed as his tongue licks me.

"Fuck, baby. You taste so damn good."

I tingle, a feeling that I thought was dead to me. My hips begin to swivel in tune with his tongue, lips, and nibbles. Hand clutching the sheets below us, my eyes close as I lose myself in the feelings.

My insides swirl and the heat in the room increases. I close my eyes, my breathing out of control. My hips arch as the climax hits me rolling through every inch of my body, waking me up from years and years of a painful sleep.

I clutch the bed hoping it'll hold me to the earth, yet also hoping I can stay far away. Waylon's touches become soft as I come back down, my eyes opening to find him watching me.

"So fuckin' beautiful."

I haven't felt beautiful in so long his words slice through my heart.

He climbs up my body. "Need to make love to you, Jess. Need you." I nod, trying to get my breathing in order. My heart going off inside me like a jackhammer.

He maneuvers his body, and I feel the brush of fabric hit my legs as his boxers disappear. Waylon looks into my eyes, the heat and passion only he has ever given me screams loud and clear. His hard tip hits my entrance, and I widen my legs for him.

His cock presses inside of me. I have wanted this. The connection is and always will be so strong between us, and I want more and more and more. It's tight. Really tight. There has been nothing inside of me for years, and it's almost as if I'm a virgin again.

"Fuck baby, we've gotta go slow."

"Please," I whimper as he presses an inch further inside my body stretching to accommodate him. His hips rock back and forth entering a bit more each time. I breathe out as he fills me and stills, sweat trickling on his forehead and a vein in his neck pulsing from the strain. He's holding back for me and while I appreciate it, I need him.

"Don't wanna hurt you," he grunts, his elbows coming to either side of my head as he looks down at me, fire burning in them.

"You won't. I want to remember."

His expression changes and something deep crosses his face. "Like this, do ya? Jessica, my angel, my everything."

The pace doesn't quicken, but I feel it. More so because he gazes into my eyes the entire time, melting my heart and searing my soul to his once more. Invisible threads wrap around both us connecting us to each other.

As we both reach our climax, we do so staring into each other's eyes.

"I don't deserve you, but I don't fuckin' care. You're mine, Jessica. Everything I am is yours. Forever."

"Forever," I whisper as the emotions are too much.

I am safe. I am complete. I am home.

**

"Wanna take a ride with me?" Waylon asks while I'm still riding the aftershocks of my morning orgasm while his dick still throbs inside me.

"Anytime, anywhere, I'll always ride with you," my voice is raspy.

His lips press to mine. "Fuck, in over my head already."

After thoroughly kissing me, he slides out and off leaving me feeling lost. Extending his hand, he helps me out of the bed and we shower before he helps me on his bike.

"Got a surprise for you."

My body and mind hum in anticipation. The ride takes a bit and we are clearly out of town when he finally turns off on a dirt road. Following the wooded drive down to the end, we stop in front of a house.

I climb off, unsure, and Waylon looks at me before lifting a key up. "Welcome home, Jess."

Tears prick behind my eyes. I shake my head. This can't be happening.

A month ago, I was chained to a bed praying I would never see Waylon again for his own safety. Now, we are together again and he has a house for us to make a home.

He takes me by the hand and leads me to the door. The locks look new as he inserts the key and opens the door.

"Paint and shit needs to be done, but want you to pick it out."

"This is where you live?" I ask, knowing we've been staying with Whitton and Roe.

"No, this is where we live."

It takes me a minute to absorb it all. "Waylon, what about your home?" I never asked him where he lives, what he does for a job. I've been so wrapped up in myself and what comes next I never thought about what it really means to get to know him. I accepted it all and took Roe's advice not to ask. "I know you have money. Roe took me to the bank. The money deposited was from you. I know it. Why give me that money and then buy a house like this?"

He smiles at me. Since he came back home to me, he's been relaxed in a way I've never experienced with him before.

"No more miscommunications. I told you I was bad for you. It was true, but you didn't listen. This love we got, it's too strong to keep us apart. As much as I tried to push you away, set you up to have a life without me. It wasn't meant to be. We are meant to be. You dreamed of fixing a house up, flipping it, whatever. You're my dream come true, Jessica. Never been another woman for me but you. This is me giving you your dreams come true."

I gasp because he remembered. He remembered my dreams from so long ago.

"Don't have a house. Lived at the clubhouse for years. Never had roots because, the truth is, without you I was half a man. Got you, got this life, got this love, and this is our home. Do with it as you wish."

I look around the space. It's quaint and rustic with years of experience. The walls currently have a yellowish tint that my guess would be from years of smoking inside of it, but the home doesn't have that smell. Instead, it smells like outside, like the windows have been left open and it's been aired out.

The living room and kitchen are one large open area with tall ceilings with wooden beams that float across to either side. The kitchen is small and cozy with everything I'd ever need to cook, except a dishwasher, but I'll gladly do those by hand.

Waylon grabs my hand and leads me through showing me a bathroom with all the necessities, an empty room and then a large room. "This is our room," he announces, and I can already envision redoing the floors. They are wood and old, but with some TLC they will be magnificent.

"This is perfect."

He pulls me close to him. "You're fuckin' perfect."

Happiness fills me and for once, that woman doesn't invade my thoughts. She's not in the back of my head whispering about unanswered prayers, devotions, or faith. She's gone.

CHAPTER 18

THIS IS LIFE AND IT'S DAMN GOOD!

TRIPLE THREAT

Jessica sits on the floor, a sander in her hand with the happiest expression on her face as she takes up the old surface on the wood. She's been the happiest I've seen her, even from all those years ago, these past few days.

We moved in minimally, just our bed, couch, TV and clothes. She wanted to get a start on the floors and have them done before we moved any other furniture in the place. She's almost done and about ready to stain.

I've asked to help, but she tells me that I'm going to be used for the heavy lifting later. I think she just enjoys doing the work and feeling like she's contributing to the household.

Jessica has expressed, many times, that she wants a job. Wants to feel independent again. While I can provide for her no doubt, I'm proud that she wants to do her part. I'm proud that she wants to take back her life and what she's meant to be. Every step she takes to live again makes me feel like it's one less hold my mother can have over her. She may not need a job for money, but the fact that she wants to get out and experience life means my mother is truly gone from our lives.

"Hey baby," I call out as her head pops up, the machine goes off, and she stares at me in the doorway.

"Hey," she says with a smile, making my cock hard as a rock.

I move into the room after shutting the door and look down at her. The floor is coming along beautifully. "It's beautiful."

"Thanks. It's coming. I'm hoping this weekend we can stain and seal."

"Sounds good."

She rises from the floor brushing her hands on her old jeans that look like they've been worn forever, but I know have not. "How was your day?"

I pull her into my body, and she wraps her arms around my neck. She's gained a little of her weight back and is filling out again, back to her old self.

"There's a job at the paper Kenderly and Andrea work at. It's full time, but it's a lower position. It's like a gopher pretty much, but you can move up if you want. Anyway, the job is yours if you want it," I tell her what Shamus told me today.

Her eyes widen. "Really? They want me?" She hadn't had much luck with finding a job, mostly because she's been out of loop for years and she's been trying to get on her feet.

"Yeah, baby. They want ya."

She hugs me tighter. "I want it. I'll take it. I have to work, Waylon, and being around Kenderly and Andrea will be great."

"Yeah, it'll be good." She's done well being around the brothers and integrating herself into my life. I wanted something for her where she'd feel comfortable, and those two women will make her feel it.

They'll also be there if Jessica feels like she can't take it or it becomes too much. But Jessica can hack it. I know it.

She looks up into my eyes. "Is this real?"

"What do ya mean?"

"Real? Like this is really happening. Our second chance at being together and living a life we were supposed to have."

My heart clenches tight. "Yeah, baby. It is."

"Then it was worth it."

Pain sears through me because I know what she means, and I hate that she feels this way. "No, you going through that wasn't in the plan."

"Waylon, I'd pray every day that you wouldn't come back. I'd pray that you'd stay as far away from that woman as possible. That I would endure to keep you safe. You standing here, me in your arms, makes it worth it because if it doesn't then all of it was worthless, and I refuse to look at it like that. That what doesn't kill us makes us stronger. It was our journey and it led us back to each other. It makes it worth it. You can choose to see it another way, but that is how I will see it. Our oceans coming back together no matter the waves, hurricanes, or rough waters trying to keep us apart. It was meant to be."

This woman. Everything she's been through because of my psychotic mother and she still looks at life like the water's in front of her.

"I love you."

Her eyes turn softer, and I feel it right in my chest. “Never a day I haven’t loved you.”

“Swear to you, on everything I am, that you will have a great life. That I will be here with you to love you every step of the way.”

Tears roll down her face. “Same here.” She rolls up on her toes and I lean down, kissing her lips. The soft kiss turns passionate, then turns desperate. My hands tear at her clothes while hers do the same to mine.

I back her against the wall, hike her up it and slip inside of her—finding my home. She is my home, and I fucking love her.

**

“HOW’S IT GOIN’?” my brother asks me from across the kitchen. He showed up ten minutes ago. Jessica ran over to find a different grit of sandpaper and when I asked her if she wanted me to go with her, she said she wanted to go by herself. Yes, she can definitely hack it.

“Fuckin’ great, Skinny. Fuckin’ great.”

He smiles, tilting the bottle of beer to his lips and taking a healthy swing. “Glad you got your head outta your ass.”

A chuckle escapes. “Me too.”

“She’s good for you. You fuckin’ light up when she’s in a room, brother. Fuckin’ happy, and that’s all I want for you.”

"Funny, cause that's what I wanted for you."

"Damn glad we both found it." He sighs deeply. "Fuck, brother. We came out on the other damn side. You think Lambardoni will call the marker anytime soon?" The worry can be read in his expression.

"Don't know. If he does, I'm a man of my word. I promise, though, I won't go it alone unless that's required, and I'll be safe."

"Got something more than me and my ugly mug to bring you back home now," he laughs.

"Hell yes. Best damn thing of my life."

He pauses for a moment contemplating. "You think she ever knew what real love was?"

"Our mother?" I ask, to which he nods.

I tense and then remember she can't touch either of us anymore. "I'm not sad she's gone. Fuckin' hated her and what she did to you. Fuckin' hated I couldn't stop it. Fuckin' hated we had no power. Fucking hated we had no control. She's better off underground."

"She is. You think that fucker Gerald put all of that in her head?"

I quirk my brow. "Ya, think? Mom was smart, but she also wasn't, if that makes sense. He was crazier than her—put them together and we're lucky we're not on some kind of drugs keepin' our shit together."

"Fuckin' hate her, brother."

"She's dead, TT. Hatin' her hurts you, not her. Know we can't forget that shit, but if we don't let it go and let it eat at us it'll fuck everything up. I'm not fuckin' Roe and me over that woman, and you need to make sure not to fuck shit up with Jessica."

"Never." The word leaves my lips instantly. No way in hell I'll let that happen. I'll do whatever I have to, to make sure it doesn't.

He sets the bottle on the kitchen counter. "Good. She's gone. He's gone. There's nothin' left of that life. Only what we choose to have. Brother, I choose to be fuckin' happy with my woman and family."

I set my bottle down. "Same."

Skinny comes up and wraps his arms around me slapping me once on the back. "Proud of you, brother. So fuckin' proud of you."

Those words right there mean the world to me.

Shamed by our past.

Scorned by the world.

Scarred by the hands of our flesh and blood.

Schooled by our ability to overcome it all and find happiness on the other side.

Fuck yeah, this is the other side, and I'm never going back.

CHAPTER 19

NOTHING WORTH HAVING COMES EASY!

Jessica

One month later

Brothers from the Rebels MC and co-workers from the Granville Journal Star are piled in Waylon and my home, spilling out into the back of the house. Food lines the kitchen counters and the six-person table that sits off to the side of it.

We got our furniture, but from the amount of people in the house, I'm thinking we should have waited to put it all in until after the party. Our party. Waylon and my house warming. A home. Him and I.

It's taken me weeks and it was extended longer because of my job, which I love. Yes, it is medial work, but I don't mind it one bit. I'm comfortable and do a great job. That's what means something to me.

The house is beautiful, and I've moved on to refurbishing furniture for it now. I found a beautiful four poster bed frame that has seen better days. Once I'm done with it, it will be gorgeous and I can't wait. It's a present for Waylon that I'd hoped to have done today, but that didn't happen so he has to wait.

"You've done a great job," Kenderly says, snagging a chip and popping it in her mouth as she looks at the cupboards and countertop.

"I did the countertops," Waylon puts in, coming up behind me and wrapping his arm around my waist. I never tire of that move. It's my favorite.

I elbow him playfully. "Yeah, he did, and he won't let me forget it."

"What does it matter?" Kenderly asks, looking between the two of us, and we smile.

"Because she wanted to do them, but it was the same time the bathroom flooring was in. She can't be two places at once, so I snuck in here and put it together."

"I appreciate your help." I did, and it was more about razzing Waylon than it was anger for him putting in the counters.

He squeezes me. "Know you do, baby."

Waylon leans down and kisses me.

"Alrighty, I'm out of here," Kenderly says, leaving.

I pull away slowly. "We should probably entertain the people."

"Nah, they can entertain themselves."

I love the way he is with me. It doesn't matter who is around us, I'm the most important person in the room. Waylon and I have our happily ever after.

Like this house, the floors, we've been marked, scratched, and worn a little uneven. We can be cleaned up, given a second chance, and come out of it beautiful. The character of a home comes through time. The character of a person comes from experiences. Waylon and I have been schooled in hard knocks, heartbreak, and miscommunication.

There was a time I prayed I would never see him again so he could have a life.

Having what we have, I'm thankful for unanswered prayers. He, nor I, could really live without the other—not in a full way. While he spent the beginning of our time together telling me to run away, I didn't listen and even in all the pain I endured to have this moment, this home, and this future with him … well, I'd do it all again.

He is everything I ever dreamed of in a man, a lover, and a partner.

CHAPTER 20

THIS IS MY REAL!

TRIPLE THREAT

Three weeks later

"LET'S RIDE," I tell my woman as she enters the living room. She smiles wide, turns and runs into the bedroom, no doubt going to get her jacket. She's been able to get clothes and essentials with her paychecks. I've offered to get her what she needs, but she's refused, only making me love her more.

"Ready!"

I had the seat changed on my bike and foot pegs added so she could be comfortable. She's saving up to buy a car. I want to give her one, but she absolutely refused and threatened to cut me off from her pussy. That's not an option. Sinking deep inside her every night is a reminder that we survived and she is with me. No way I will lose that.

This has been a whirlwind. My life has ended up so much different than I ever imagined. I still don't know how Lambardoni got the information on my mother, but to have Jessica safe and with me, the details don't much matter.

We are still working on getting in touch with Jessica's mom. If things go well today, then my plan is a trip to her mother's house. The woman can't avoid talking to her daughter if she's in her face. No matter what it takes, how long, or what I have to do, I will help Jessica have the relationship back with both her parents.

She climbs on and settles in.

Home.

Complete.

Whole.

Love.

I thought the open road was my freedom. It doesn't touch the way I feel with her arms wrapped around me and her body pressed to mine while my Harley roars underneath us. This is the shit no one can touch. The moments that matter.

We stop by the lake and like every other time, I wrap my arms around Jessica until she gets her legs back under her. It takes time and a lot of riding to really get used to the jelly feeling when you first get off a bike. Mostly, I just love holding her close. In fact, I hope twenty years from now she still needs this so I can always be the one to hold her up and hold her steady.

"I'm good," she whispers, looking out over the water. The sun is getting low on the horizon and with our location, it will hit right when the sun goes over and hopefully will shine on the water. Perfect.

I dig in the saddlebag and pull out the blanket, then take her hand and we walk out to the edge of the water facing the sun. Spreading it out, I lay, then pull Jessica down between my legs so her back is to my front.

“This is nice.” Jessica melts into me. I hold her close as ducks fly into the water making a huge splash. Jessica laughs, and it’s music to my ears.

We watch the ducks dive under the water, then prune their feathers. Everything is peaceful. Right. Calm. The fucking life that I want. She is what I want. Forever.

The sun falls to the horizon, and I pull the ring out of my pocket, reach for Jessica’s hand, and slip it on her finger.

She gasps, turning in my arms.

“Love you. Now and forever. You’re my ride or die, and I’ll spend the rest of my days making sure you’re happy, loved, and taken care of. Marry me.”

She moves fast wrapping her arms around my neck, pushing me to the ground on my back. “Yes. There is nothing I want more!”

She kisses me and gives me everything, including her heart and soul—forever.

Peace. I find my peace.

EXCERPT OF BLOOD AND LOYALTIES BY RYAN MICHELE

Blood & Loyalties: A Mafia Romance by Ryan Michele

CHAPTER ONE

Catarina

"YOU STUPID FUCKING bitch!" Antonio seethed like a pussy as he looked up from the filthy-ass floor of the bar, holding his throbbing crotch.

I laughed, tossing my head back for good measure. Bitch was the worst he could come up with? I had been called worse than that at work when I lost a client's millions on a bum deal.

I lifted the pointed heel of my black, stiletto boot and plowed it hard into his windpipe, crushing it as he gasped for breath, his eyes wide with fear. He needed to be taught a lesson about fucking over a Lambardoni. It didn't come without repercussions, and I wanted to be the one to teach him.

Unfortunately, I knew my bodyguards had called my brother Val. They always did when shit with me happened, and if I didn't get on with it, Val would ruin all my fun. I was more than capable of handling this weak, pathetic asshole. Val should know that. He and my other brother D had trained me to fight and shoot a target with precision, but something about being "the sister" gave them the right to be overprotective and overbearing, even if I was older than both of them.

As I removed my foot, one of his hands wrapped around his throat as the other continued to grip his aching crotch. The stupid fucker didn't know whether to grab his balls or neck, his arms flailing in both directions as he rolled from side to side, trying to ease the pain. He gasped for breath, the look of confusion in his eyes laughable. I did pack one hell of a powerful knee thrust, though. No doubt his balls were shoved so deep inside he could taste them in his mouth.

Wicked thoughts crept in my head. Using my best weapon of the moment—the hot ass boots my cousin Kiera had insisted I wear for the night—I picked a spot on his rib cage and began kicking it over and over, plowing into him, hoping like hell the blows would crack the fuckers. It was the least he deserved.

I moved with him at each turn he tried to make, hitting him dead in the same spot. He grunted and attempted to bat my foot away with his hands as he tried to hold himself at the same time. His less than stealthy attempts only made him look like a bigger pansy-assed bitch. It was amazing how much actual joy I felt from watching him struggle.

He tried to curl up in the fetal position, the dirt from the floor coating his clothes and both sides of his face. He groaned, taking each hit, but it didn't feel like enough. The fucker didn't even have the balls to really fight back.

"Catarina, what the hell happened?" Kiera said loudly at my side, trying to compensate for the music blaring in the distance. She was my cousin, best friend, and pretty much sister in every way that counts. Regardless, my focus stayed on the fucker on the floor as I stepped farther back from his withering body.

When Kiera and I had decided to come out to the club to let off some steam from a brutal week at work, I hadn't realized I would be getting a hefty workout like this instead of on the dance floor.

I stared down at the man I'd thought loved me, who had said I was the one for him. The *only* one. Stupid. I should have known by now that the only reason men found any interest in me was because of my father and family. Each one seemed to want that pivotal "in" to the business, and for some reason, they thought I could get it for them.

I knew Antonio wanted to move up in the ranks with his family, but it wasn't in the cards for him. That right there should have been a huge red flag for me, but I had trusted him when he told me if he couldn't move up in his own family, he didn't want to move up at all.

Lies. All fucking lies. One would think I had learned this lesson after twenty-nine years on this earth, but I kept falling for it: hook, line, and sinker. The word sucker was plastered on my fucking forehead, and the life that I craved so much was completely unobtainable. Not anymore. This would be it. This fucker would be the absolute last.

Being the daughter of a very powerful man came with a stiff price, the biggest being whom to trust, which I had learned—mostly the hard way—wasn't many. Family was about the only ones I could, and damn if that didn't suck ass with finding a love life.

Even women had proved too scarce in the honesty department. Most wanting to fuck my brothers rather than actually get to know me. That was why Kiera and I had stuck together over the years. It was safer for everyone. No one else understood this life.

I wasn't and never had been a weak person. Growing up in the Lambardoni family, it wasn't an option. Between my father, uncle, brothers, and cousins, both Kiera and I had been taught with an iron fist—a loving iron fist—but still, a strong-gripping fist.

Glancing down at the floor, I couldn't believe I had wasted my time on this man. I would have to thank my brother Dominic—D—for teaching me kickboxing. It proved handy, even if my technique was shit at the moment, but it was kind of hard to really show technique when the guy was on the ground.

The asshole growling under my feet thought he could profess his undying love for me and then go fuck some blonde whore in the bathroom. Mistake. Big mistake.

When he told me he was going to get drinks then headed in the opposite way of the bar, every flag in my head stood to alert. Val had taught me how to observe one's surroundings, promising me it would come in handy one day, and that day was definitely one of them.

Throughout Val's teachings, my eyes became sharper in viewing my surroundings and noticing key things that were out of place: a car parked somewhere it shouldn't be or a person walking a bit too closely. I'd see it, and it would keep me on my toes.

Realizing Antonio turned down the hallway in his quest for drinks, I'd motioned for my full-time guard, Scraper—yes, that was his name—to follow him. He took off, only to report back minutes later that Antonio had a piece of ass in the women's bathroom.

The pained expression on Scraper's face sent me into action. I knew it was pained because of the betrayal to me, and I would be putting Antonio's ass on a stick.

I rushed through the crowd with Scraper on my heels, trying to get through the crush of people. I knew Scraper would stay out of the confrontation until or if he needed to intervene. He had been my guard for the past six years, and while at first we couldn't stand the sight of each other, he'd grown on me over the years. After growing up together, I even liked him, and he knew when to step back and let me take the lead so I could prove myself capable to my family, which was a must.

I'd caught a glimpse through the crack in the door of that piece of shit, confirming he was in fact balls deep in pussy that wasn't mine, and then I waited. I was exceptionally patient, one of my many redeeming qualities. As I stood back in the shadows of the darkened, narrow hallway that led to the bathroom, I tried reining in my anger. It would get me nowhere and cause me to make stupid mistakes. Having a clear head was the only way to go. Hurt had already gone out the damn window. There was no need for that or any other emotion.

Scraper had stayed on the other side as my back-up. He knew the fucker had to pay, exactly as I did. It would actually just be the start of his repercussions. Once my brothers, cousins, and—God help him—father and uncle heard, he would get a hell of a lot worse than what I was about to dish out. It was probably demented, but I was actually happy about that.

After the blonde whore left, swaying her fake ass down the hallway, Antonio came strutting out like the cat who got his mouse. There had been a wide smile across his face and even a bead of sweat on his brow. Before he could see me, I'd lifted my knee with every ounce of power I could muster in my five-foot-ten body and kneed him in his balls. He hunched over, and I helped him to the floor by kicking his legs out from under him. He plummeted to the ground hard, his shoulder taking the weight of the fall. Stupid fuck.

"Just handling some trash. Caught him fucking some blonde in the bathroom," I said to Kiera, whose beautiful face turned glacial in seconds. The smooth skin around her eyes narrowed with lines as she released a heavy breath.

Kiera lifted the heel of her beautiful, hot pink pumps and smashed them into Antonio's nose, causing blood to splatter at my feet and across the floor. I had been going for no blood, but shit happened.

"Dammit, I just got these boots, too." I pretended to whine, stomping my foot for added emphasis. In actuality, I couldn't give a shit. I would go buy new ones tomorrow.

Never in my life had I wanted for anything, but don't think for a moment that I hadn't worked for every penny of it. In my family, you learned very early on everything you got, you worked hard for. Your blood, sweat, and tears went into every dollar you spent; hence, why Kiera and I wanted a fun night out, hoping to get a reprieve from life. Life had other ideas, though.

"We'll shop tomorrow," Kiera spat down on Antonio as he started shrieking nasty names at us. Some in Italian, some in English. I ignored him as I hacked up a wad and spit it down on his worthless body.

Spitting on someone in my family was the formal yet disgusting sign of a person being dead to you. If someone was trash and unworthy of you, you spit. It was pretty damn gross, but people understood it and normally asked no questions once it was done. If they did, they were more than likely going to get the shit beat out of them again. In Antonio's case, I hoped he would, just for fun.

"All right, ladies. It's done." Scraper slid up to us and rested his hands on our shoulders, giving a slight, comforting squeeze.

I wasn't quite ready to give it up. The tension in my body was still wound tight and needed release, but I looked over to Kiera who nodded in agreement, deflating my plans.

Kiera was always my voice of reason. It was why we worked so well together. We complimented each other to a T.

"The boys will be here soon to clean up. Let's go get you ladies a drink," Scraper said with another squeeze as we stepped farther back, and I tried to pull out of my tension.

Antonio tried hard to stand, his feet and knees wobbling underneath him as he groaned in pain with each movement. He was able to partially get up, but he was bent at the waist and kept shifting from one foot to the other, like either one he chose hurt too much to put his full weight on.

"I'll fucking kill you for this, bitch!" Antonio snapped at me. He didn't seem to understand the concept of '*you just got your ass handed to you, so shut the fuck up*.'

Scraper pulled both Kiera and I behind him then landed a hard punch to Antonio's jaw. The loud crack echoed through the hall, even over all the boisterous music playing. Antonio's eyes rolled into the back of his head as he fell onto the floor, his head landing with an audible thud on the tile. His body was unmoving from what I hoped was just being passed out. I didn't need to explain this man's death to my father or uncle.

"Come. Now," Scraper commanded, looking down at the piece of shit. "Or else a bullet goes through the fucker's head."

I rolled my eyes. While I knew he would totally do it, I also knew he would pick a more discreet location than right by the bathroom in a bar. Too many witnesses. Even though no one was around us at the moment, a gunshot would surely bring everyone running.

"Let me wash up." I didn't wait for a response from either of them, entering the bathroom to clean off Antonio once and for all. I hated having Antonio's blood on me in any way, even on my shoes.

Months of my life were wasted on that piece of shit, time I would never get back. I sighed, wishing things had been different. I thought he might have actually been *the one*. Who was I shitting? The one, my ass. He didn't exist for me.

After I was done, I stepped out of the bathroom to a waiting Kiera and Scraper.

"Come on, girl. I'm thirsty." I needed to get something inside of me to calm the hyped up feeling I had coursing through my veins. Love it or hate it, the crash from adrenaline usually sucked, and I wanted to be drunk when it happened. Forgetting seeing Antonio and that whore fucking was an added bonus.

"I bet you are," Kiera giggled, grabbing my arm and pulling me back up to the VIP section.

Scraper led the way up the side stairs, but I could feel Dune and Case behind us. They were Kiera's guards. She had two because of the whole being the daughter of the great Vino Lambardoni thing. We each had two other guards who we called Ghost One and Ghost Two. We had met them there, but they hid in the shadows, only coming out when necessary, which was seldom. They were there yet not there. It was eerie in a way, but we got used to it like everything else.

I couldn't remember a time in my life when she and I hadn't had guards of some sort tailing our every movement. Most would say it wasn't normal, but what the hell was normal, anyway? Our fathers did it for our safety, and we accepted that. Although I'm not saying back in the day we hadn't tried to ditch them and escape the confines of our fathers.

I laughed thinking about it. We had been so dumb and had no understanding of what kinds of threats were out there for us. We were honest to God lucky nothing had happened to us.

Music thumped through the large speakers while men and women shook their asses and everything else they had on the dance floor below us. All of them were oblivious to what just occurred in the back of the bar, which was perfect, easier to clean up. It was also a sure sign life went on even in the midst of someone's mistakes.

Scraper led us to the plush red velvet chairs with the white trim in our closed off room. We took a seat in the dimly lit space where glass mirrored walls lined the front, allowing a great view of the bar and dance floor.

The waitress with her tight red and white shirt and barely there black shorts approached hastily after we were seated. "What can I get ya, ladies?"

The perkiness of the woman's voice made me want to wretch. I had been a lot of things in my life, but perky was not one of them, and I was seriously not in the mood for a bubbly cheerleader. I let it go, however, ignoring it.

"Shots!" Both Kiera and I said together then smiled, looking at each other knowingly. I loved how we could always read each other's minds. Sometimes it was a bit scary when we could do it from across the room.

"Patrón, please. Just bring the bottle, glasses, and limes," I said.

She nodded, rushing off down the stairs with Dune's eyes latched on to her ass. Men.

Kiera leaned back in the chair, her eyes flickering around, surveying our surroundings. She had a radiant beauty about her. Her long, chestnut brown hair in a shade or two different than my own flowed down her back. She had brown eyes with golden specks flashing inside of them, so different than my bluish-green eyes. She drew in any man she wanted, but rarely did she take a guy up on his propositions. She was happy with herself just the way she was, and I loved her dearly.

With Scraper at the entrance of the VIP area, Dune and Case made themselves at home on the other side of the small space, leaning against the wall, mirroring each other with arms crossed over their chests.

We loved having our own area up here. It gave us the opportunity to dance when we wanted and then get away without anyone bothering us unless we wanted them to. It was no secret who we were—personally or professionally—but neither of us ever let that shit go to our heads.

"Antonio had the fucking balls to screw some chick while he was here with you?" Kiera broke the silence between us, obviously not done talking about what had happened. In truth, I wasn't done, either. I needed to get shit out and calm the hell down.

I chuckled even though I didn't find any part of it a bit funny; it was just what came out with an evil death twinge to it. "Stupid, huh? And he must have set it up ahead of time because he wanted to make it quick. There's no way he just picked this chick up tonight. He was in there less than five minutes. I should feel bad for the woman, but I don't. He never could keep it up long. Loser," I growled with the laughter. He always had been fast to the punch, but it was one of those things I'd overlooked.

"I thought you said he was good in bed?" She raised her eyebrow in question, staring at me. I had never lied to Kiera and never would.

I shrugged. "Define good. He made me come. Was it mind-blowing? Fuck no, but he made me feel good, told me I was beautiful, blah, blah, blah. He acted like he wasn't afraid of my dad or brothers beating the shit out of him, but who the hell knows?" I wondered if all of that was a lie, too. More than likely, yes.

"Dumbass. He should have worried about you," Kiera said with another slight giggle.

She had seen my handiwork over the years. Some of it was a bit overdone, but I always had a purpose, like tonight. I wasn't one of those women who were lovers and not fighters. While I wanted to be, I was more the opposite. I always blamed it on my brothers because I sure as shit didn't want to blame myself.

"No shit there." I laughed for real this time. Everyone, including my family, sometimes underestimated me. It worked out in my favor, though. I was a snake—lethal when you pissed me off and would strike when you least expected it. "What a fucking pussy. Did you see him?" I rolled my eyes, waving my hand, unable to help myself. "I didn't realize how big of one he was until tonight." Antonio didn't come off to me like that for all the months I had known him. He had always been a standup guy, even to my father. It was like he did a one-eighty.

"Sorry, babe." Her arm snaked around my shoulders, and she pulled me to her side, giving me a squeeze as I leaned into her comforting touch. The compassion she gave me filled my heart.

If anything, I knew I would always have her by my side. We might grow old and gray together because no man had the balls to step up to either of our fathers, but we would have each other.

The waitress flounced back into the room, setting glasses full of clear liquid, the bottle, and a bowl of limes onto the small table in front of us. Kiera released me, leaned over, and handed me a shot while taking one for herself. Then she held it high in the air, and I followed. She was clearly in a toasting mood tonight. Fine by me.

"To one day finding Mr. Right who loves to eat pussy and not be one!"

I laughed hard at her words, clinking my glass to hers and watching the clear liquid sway around the glass. We tossed back the shot in unison, and I felt the burn race down my throat then splash into my stomach. I sucked on a lime and squinted at the sourness on my tongue, already thinking it was time for another.

If anything, Kiera's love life was worse than mine when it came to her family. With her dad—my Uncle Vino—being the head of the family, guys flocked to her, too, but their main goal was to be with the boss's daughter, marry her, and then take over the business. At least with my dad as second in command, it wasn't as bad.

Who was I fucking kidding? We were both doomed.

Several shots and some serious lime sucking later, our laughter billowed all around us. My body relaxed, and the tension from *the asshole* melted away.

I scanned the joint, seeing if there were any potential men in the crowd—hey, I was a free woman now—but none were calling to me. Maybe it was just me. Getting laid had never been the problem; it was all the other shit in my life that came into play. After the night I'd had, I wasn't feeling it all that much.

There might not be potential men, but that was a moot point as my brother Val, his best friend Ace, and a man I had never seen before—but holy hell would like to see more of—entered the VIP section. I breathed out deeply and quickly turned away from the handsome man, my body fluttering by merely being in the same room as him.

What was wrong with me? Men didn't do this to me. Ever. My eyes connected with my brother's, whose tight brows, sky blue eyes glaring, and thin-lined mouth told me he was pissed as shit. Too damn bad. I was too drunk to care.

"What mess did you get yourself into this time?" Val asked in a clipped tone. Most people would probably fall at his feet and pray for mercy or cower in a corner at that tone. Me? Not so much.

Being my younger brother by two years, he thought it was his job to protect me. For some reason, he thought he was the older sibling and took the overprotective brother thing to another level. Too bad he was wrong.

Val and I were almost carbon copies of each other, with the same dark hair and golden-toned skin. The only difference was Val had blue eyes, while I had ones that were sometimes blue and sometimes green. It simply depended on the lighting. Even with his more rough and demanding features, no one would mistake that we were siblings.

I waved him off, flicking my hand in the air because nothing would tap down his anger. It was too raw in his eyes. Whenever something went badly that involved me, he had serious issues. God love him, but he needed to calm the hell down.

I leaned back in the chair and took a sip of the cranberry juice and patron I'd had the waitress bring a while ago. "Scraper's handling the cleanup. No big deal," I told him. It was over and done with, and Scraper had guys taking care of the rest.

"Bullshit. That asshole fucks some bitch in a bathroom while he's dating *my*"—he pointed his finger to his chest and pressed firmly for emphasis—"sister. I'll handle this shit," he growled deeply, the veins in his head throbbing and his face turning beet red. He was seriously going to have a heart attack before he reached thirty at this rate. He needed to relax and not let this shit get to him so bad.

"No need. He learned his lesson. If he didn't and comes after me, I'll take care of it." I took another drink, feeling maybe a little bit cocky, letting the liquid bounce to my stomach, but by then it didn't give me any aftereffects.

I had every bit of confidence in myself that I would be able to handle whatever situation came up. Even drunk, I could deal.

"Hey, Val," Kiera greeted, breaking up the thick tension that was spiraling out of control from my brother. "Take a breath, boy."

Kiera was my age, only younger by three months, but that didn't matter with her brothers, either. She dealt with this same shit, so she understood. She normally would have a calming effect on my brother, which she had on most people, but not so much this time.

Val turned to Kiera with the same fury, but he lightened up just a tad. "Kiera, your dad's gonna be pissed you're in this shit." He pointed at both of us with a hostile glare, his eyes darting between the two of us. "You know he's part of the Capella family."

Since rolling my eyes at him and yelling duh was way too immature, I decided against it. "No shit, Sherlock. I don't care." It was my turn to growl at my brother. Family was family. If the Capella's had a problem, they could deal with their own fuck-up of a member. Not my problem.

"There's a meeting in a few days with Remeo. This will not go well." Val shook his head, grabbing the back of his neck. Remeo was the head of Antonio's family.

"It's not my fault his dick didn't stay in his pants. He got what he deserved." He had, but I was sure I would hear from my father about this and maybe Uncle Vino. However, I wouldn't change what I had done to that sorry ass. I was only a little pissed at myself for allowing him to leave with his balls still intact.

"Dammit, you think I don't know that? I just hate this drama shit." I couldn't see any of the men in my life being pissed at me. If anything, they would rip Antonio apart, so I was in the clear for the most part. Business-wise, I didn't work alongside any of them to know what that outcome would be.

"Hi, Ace." I winked at the man who's been by my brother's side since we were kids.

"Hey, babe. How you been?" Ace's sexy voice fell over the room as he slowly walked closer to me.

I wouldn't deny for a second that I found Ace dreamy as shit. With his dark hair, deep chocolate eyes, and a body built like an Italian rock, I throbbed every time I saw the man. Problem was, he had a girl and had since high school—Beth.

"Great. Who's your friend?" I nodded toward him, sweeping my gaze over to the man with sharp denim eyes boring holes right through me, sending shivers down my spine.

Now Ace was hot, but this guy tipped the hot-o-meter by another twenty plus. Broad shoulders pulled his V-neck, black shirt tight, showing every ripple underneath of muscular perfection and giving a glimpse of a slight dusting of dark chest hair. Not the long kind, but the kind that looks like he cut it short, and it was sexy as hell. Tattoos lined his arms and snuck under the sleeves of his shirt, making my mouth water from wanting to lick up and down every muscle. His face was like something chiseled from a damn sculpture, and his beard and slight stash made my thighs quiver. I wouldn't mind a little rug burn.

"This is Jag."

Jag's eyes continued to set me on fire as they raked up and down my body, taking in every inch of me. I was not a small woman, but I had been told my curves were what set me apart from others. All ass and tits, one man had told me. Even better, I loved every one of them.

"You done eye-fucking me?" I boldly asked, smirking, before hearing my brother's exasperated sigh beside me.

"Not yet." His deep baritone voice glided over my skin like a silky glove just waiting to slide on. His terse words caused every sense in my body to come to full alert, and the hair rose on the back of my neck like a shock wave. My heart pounded in my chest, but I kept my breathing slow, not allowing any signs show.

"No, she's my sister. Off limits," my brother said.

I turned and glared at him, standing with my hip cocked and my hand resting on it. "Don't you dare, Val. No wonder the only men I hook up with are fucking douches."

My brother gave nothing except fury at my words that had never been truer. I could name five guys off the top of my head whom Val had played a role in making disappear from my life, and I'd had enough.

Val stepped in my space, getting close to my face, his hot breath bouncing off my nose. "What the hell is that supposed to mean? I told your ass to get rid of Antonio as soon as I heard you were dating him."

I stared, my nostrils flaring in rebellion, clenching my fists at my sides. Not the most attractive sight, but it got my don't-fuck-with-me vibe going. The sad thing was, it hadn't intimidated him since we were kids, but I refused to be walked over.

"I was hoping it would work. I was wrong. Better I learned that for my damn self instead of my overbearing brother getting in my damn business every time I turn around!" My voice rose, bringing more attention to our conversation as the guards took a step forward. "What the hell do you want from me? Just to live with Kiera for the rest of my life, have random fucks with men, and never find my one?" I had lost control by letting the last part slip out, but it was out there. Time to deal.

"First, no random fucks. Ever."

I blew out an exasperated breath, trying to calm myself as I ran my fingers through my hair, pulling it tersely.

"Second, living with Kiera keeps you both safe. Third, what the fuck is this 'one' bullshit? Don't tell me your little clock is ticking, and you need to find a man." He chuckled sardonically, actually making fun of me.

Blood boiled in my veins as I stepped closer. Even with my heels, I had to tilt my head to connect with his eyes. I needed to get my point across and have his full, undivided attention. Inside, I vibrated, pulsing with anger that fled through every cell of my body, eating away at me like a virus.

"This damn bubble you and Daddy have me in is about to burst. I am a grown-ass woman you all have taught well. I run a damn business with Kiera, so I am not fucking stupid. Antonio was a poor choice, but with your dictation, my choices are pretty damn limited. I'm sick of this shit. Done. You keep this up and you will not like the results." I stepped away.

Our close-knit group was quiet, waiting for his reaction, but I didn't wait for it, didn't care what it was.

"I'm leaving," I announced to the room, moving to the door, the alcohol no longer having a hold on me. Fights with Val always seemed to sober me.

"Scraper," I called to the man still standing at the entrance of the VIP, his arms crossed, looking mean.

He nodded yet said nothing as I grabbed my purse from the red velvet chair and looked into Kiera's glowing eyes filled with concern.

"Sorry, babe. I just can't do this anymore. You coming or you gonna stay?"

"I've gotta go meet with my brothers. I just got a text." She held up her phone, dangling it in front of me. "I'll be home in a bit." Compassion laced her eyes, but she knew I had been on the brink of my family's meddling for a while now. The breaking point had to come sometime.

She nodded, calling her guards over as she walked out of the small room with them.

"Wait." My brother scowled, grabbing my arm tightly and pulling on me.

I yanked it back as I seethed with anger. How dare his ass put his hands on me?

"Get. Your. Hands. Off. Me." I bit out with what was left of my self-control, but he didn't relent. Instead, he pulled me more firmly to him, making me gasp and no doubt leaving a mark on my body.

"You know we love you. We just want to protect you. If you'd listen to what we said about Antonio, I wouldn't be here, cleaning up your fucking mess."

A red, hazy film covered my eyes as I used every ounce of strength to rip my arm out of his firm grasp. He stood there in shock, looking at his hand like he couldn't believe I had actually been able to get away from him. Apparently, I was stronger than I looked. He'd do best to remember that.

"You go clean up my mess, brother," I snapped even though Scraper had said it was handled. I was just pissed he had made the comment in the first place. "That is your job, after all," I sassed, leaving quickly with Scraper and my Ghost—who had come into play during the altercation—on my heels.

I just caught the smirk that played on Jag's face as I breezed by him and Ace.

Outside, Scraper opened the car door for me, and I climbed into the passenger seat of the sleek, black automobile, feeling the coolness of the leather on my thighs. It did nothing to cool down the raging inferno inside of me, though. I only wanted to go home.

I replayed the night in my head on a loop, the alcohol simmering in my veins. My brother was at the forefront of the raging thoughts. He couldn't expect me to continue on like this, being under his thumb, crushing me. He had flat out told Jag I was off limits. What right did he have to do that? None.

Before I could finish my thoughts, we were home.

EXCERPT OF IN THE RED BY CHELSEA CAMARON

Prologue

I hang my head and sit in silence. The television blares as strangers move about our house. Some of them are trying to put together a search party, and others are here with food and weak attempts to comfort. I want them all to go away so I can scream or break something. I want each and every one of them to stop looking at me like I should be beaten within an inch of my life then allowed to heal, only to get beaten again. Do I deserve that?

Hell yes, I do, and more.

There is no reprieve from this hell we are in. I would sell my soul to the Devil himself if I could turn back time. Only, I can't.

The reporter's voice breaks through all of the clamor.

"In local news tonight, a nine-year-old girl is missing, and authorities are asking for your help. Raleigh Ragnes was last seen by her seventeen-year-old brother. According to her parents, he was watching Raleigh after school when the child wandered outside and down the street on her pink and white bicycle with streamers on the handlebars.

"Raleigh was last known to have her brown hair braided in two braids with a yellow ribbon tied at the

bottom of each. She wore a yellow shirt under a black denim dress that went to her knees. She wore white Keds with two different color laces: one pink and the other purple.

"There is a reward offered for any information leading to the successful return of Raleigh to her home. Any information is appreciated and can be given by calling the local sheriff's department."

The television seems to screech on and on with other reports as if our world hasn't just crumbled. My mom's sobs only grow louder.

God, I'm an ass. Raleigh was whining all afternoon about going to Emerson's house. Those two are practically inseparable. She had made the trip numerous times to the Flint's home at the end of the cul-de-sac, so I didn't think twice about her leaving.

Since Gretchen was here, we were locked in my room, doing things that didn't involve studying or thinking about my kid sister. The more Raleigh asked to leave, the more Gretchen would get distracted. I knew I had to get her gone or suffer the worst case of blue balls I could imagine. My hand was just making it down her pants when I yelled at Raleigh through the door to just go, not wanting the distraction. Not once did I give a second thought to her leaving.

Only, while I was making my way to home base, my little sister never made it to her friend's house. None of us knew until dinner time that my sister had never come home. The phone call to Emerson's sent us all into a tailspin.

While other families watch the eleven o'clock news to simply be informed, tonight, for my family, my little sister is the news.

~Three weeks later ~

The television screeches once again. I thought the world had crumbled before, but now it's crushed beyond repair. The reporter's tone is not any different than if she were giving the local weather as the words crash through my ears.

"In local news tonight, the body of nine-year-old Raleigh Ragnes was found in a culvert pipe under Old Mill Road. Police are asking for anyone with any information to please come forward. The case is being treated as an open homicide."

In the matter of a month, my sister went from an innocent little girl to a case number, and in time, she will be nothing more than a file in a box. Everyone else may have called it cold and left it unsolved, but that's not who I am. The ease in which they gave up on her molded my entire future. Detective O'Malley broke the news that they were giving up, and I made the decision I would give my life to finding the guilty party, no matter the cost.

The domino effect of one person's crime going unpunished is beyond measure.

Chapter One

~Dover~

Giving up is not an option for me. It never has been.

"There's a time and a place to die, brother," I say, scooping Trapper's drunk ass off the dirty floor of the bar with both my hands under his armpits. "This ain't it."

The bar we are in is a hole in the wall joint, the kind we find in small towns everywhere. It's a step above a shack on the outside, and the inside isn't much better: one open room, linoleum floor from the eighties. The bar runs the length of the space with a pair of saloon-style swinging doors closing off the stock room. We have gotten shit-faced in nicer, and we have spent more than our fair share in worse.

At the end of a long ride, a cold beer is a cold beer. Really, it doesn't matter to us where it's served as long as the brew has been on ice and is in a bottle.

"I'm nowhere near dying," he slurs, winking at the returning from the bathroom. Waiting and watching for her to return to his lap is how he fell to the floor. She's another no name come guzzler in a slew of many we find throughout every city, town, and stop we make. "In fact, I'm not far from showing sweet thing here a little piece of heaven."

"Trapper." Judge, the calmest of us all, gets in his face. "She rode herself to oblivion. Until you fell off the stool, she might have come back for a round two. She's done got hers, man. Time to get you outta here so you can have some quality time huggin' Johnny tonight."

We all laugh as Trapper tries to shake me off.

"Fuck all y'all. That pussy is mine tonight."

"Shithead, sober up. She's headed to the bathroom again to snort another line, and she won't be coming back for another ride on your thigh. Time to go, brother," Rowdy says sternly as we watch the broad make her way the restrooms. Rowdy was ready to leave an hour ago. This isn't his scene.

Trapper turns to the long-haired, six-foot-six man of muscle and gives him a shit-eating grin. "Aw, Rowdy, are you gonna be my sober sister tonight?"

I wrap my arm around Trapper, pulling him into a tight hold. "Shut your mouth now!"

He holds up his hands in surrender, and we make our way out of the bar.

Another night, another dive. Tomorrow is a new day and a new ride.

Currently, we are in Leed, Alabama for a stop off. The green of the trees, the rough patches of the road, like every other place—it all does nothing to bring any of us out of the haunting darkness we each carry.

We are nomads with no place to call home, and that's how we like it. The six of us have been a club of our own creation for a few years now. We each have a story to tell. We all have a reason we do what we do. None of us are noble or honorable. We strike in the most unlikely of places and times, all based on our own brand of rules and systems.

Fuck the government. Fuck their laws. And damn sure fuck the judicial system.

Once your name is tainted, no matter how good you are, you will never be clean in the eyes of society. I'm walking, talking, can't sleep at night proof of it. Well, good fucking deal. I have learned society's version of clean is everything I don't ever want to be.

The scum that blends into our communities and with our children, the cons that can run a game, they think they are untouchable. The number of crimes outnumber the crime fighters. The lines between law abiding and law breaking blur every day inside every precinct. I know because I carried the badge and thought I could be a change in the world. Then I found out everything is just as corrupt for the people upholding the law as those breaking it.

Day in and day out, watching cops run free who deserve to be behind bars more than the criminals they put away takes its toll. Everyone has a line in the sand, and once they cross it, they don't turn back. I found mine. Then I found the brotherhood in the Devil's Due MC. Six guys who have all seen our own fair share of corruption in the justice system. Six guys who don't give a fuck about the consequences.

Well, that's where me and my boys ride in. No one's above the devil getting his due. We are happy to serve up our own kind of punishments that most certainly fit the crimes committed, and we don't bother with the current legal system's view of justice served.

Wayward souls, damaged men who have nothing more than vengeance on our minds, we ride as six with no ties to anyone or anything from one city to the next. We have a bond. We are the only family for each other, and we keep it that way. No attachments, no commitments, and that means no casualties.

We are here by choice. Any man can leave the club and our life behind at any time. I trust these men with my life and with my death. When my time is called, they will move on with the missions as they come.

"Fucking bitch got my pants wet," Trapper says, just realizing she really did get off on his thigh and left him behind. "You see this shit?" He points at his leg.

Trapper mad is good. He'll become focused rather than let the alcohol keep him in a haze. He could use some time to dry up. He's sharp. His attention to detail saves our asses in city after city. However, things get too close to home when we ride to the Deep South like this, and he can't shake the ghosts in the closets of his mind. At five-foot-ten and a rock solid one eighty-five, he's a force of controlled power. He may be drunk, yet once the wind hits his face, he'll be solid. He always is. He uses his brain more than his brawn, but he won't back down in a brawl, either.

We help him get outside the dive bar we spent the last two hours inside, tossing beer back and playing pool. Outside, the fresh winter air hits him, and he shakes his head.

"It's not that cold," X says, slapping Trapper in the face. "Sober up, sucka."

Trapper smiles as he starts to ready his mind. As drunk as he is, he knows he has to have his head on straight to ride.

"Flank him on either side, but stay behind in case he lays her down. We only have four miles back to the hotel," I order, swinging my leg over my Harley Softail Slim and cranking it. The rumble soothes all that stays wound tight inside me. The vibration reminds me of the power under me.

Blowing out a breath, I tap the gas tank. "Ride for Raleigh," I whisper and point to the night sky. *Never forget*, I remind myself before I move to ride. With my hands on the bars, twisting the throttle, I let the bike move me and lift my feet to rest on the pegs.

As each of my brother's mount, I pull out and relax as the road passes under me, knowing they will hit the throttle and catch me.

At the no-tell motel we are crashing at, X takes Trapper with him to one of the three shit-ass rooms we booked while Judge and Rowdy go to the other. The place has seen better days, probably thirty years ago. It's a place to shit, shower, and maybe sleep if I can keep the nightmares away. I have never needed anything fancy, and tonight is no different.

I give them a half-salute as they close their doors and lock down for the night.

Deacon heads on into our room. Always a man of few words and interaction, he doesn't look back or give me any indication that he cares if I follow or stay behind.

I give myself the same moment I take every night to stand out under the stars and smoke.

I look up. Immediately, I can hear her tiny voice in my mind, making up constellations all her own. Raleigh was once a rambunctious little girl afraid of nothing. She loved the night sky and wishing upon all the stars.

Another city, another life, I wish it was another time, but one thing I know is that there is no turning back time. If I could, I would. Not just for me, but for all six of us.

I light my cigarette and take a deep drag. Inhaling, I hold it in my lungs before I blow out. The burn, the taste, and the touch of it to my lips don't ease the thoughts in my mind. Another night is upon us, and it's yet another night Raleigh will never come home.

The receptionist from the hotel lobby steps out beside me. She isn't the one who was here when we checked in earlier. However, when she smiles up at me, I can tell she has been waiting on us. Guess the trailer trash from day shift chatted up her replacement. Well, at least this one has nice teeth. Day shift definitely doesn't have dental on her benefit plan here.

"Go back inside," I bark, not really in the mood for company.

"I'm entitled to a break," she challenges with a southern drawl.

"If you want a night with a biker, I'm not the one," I try to warn her off.

"Harley, leather, cigarettes, and sexy—yeah, I think you're the one … for tonight, that is." She comes over and reaches out for the edges of my cut.

I grab her wrists. "You don't touch my cut," I growl in frustration. She is playing with fire and seems to get off on it, biting her bottom lip with a sly smile.

There is a rasp to her tone as she tries for seduction. “Oh, rules. I can play by the rules, big daddy.”

I drop her hands and walk in a circle around her before standing in front of her then backing her toward the wall. I take another drag of my cigarette and blow the smoke into her face. “I’m not your fucking daddy.” I take another long drag. Smoke blows out with each word as I let her know, “If you wanna fuck, we’ll fuck. Make no mistake, though, I’m not in the mood to chat, cuddle, or kiss. I’ll fuck, and that’s it.”

She leans her head back, testing me.

“Hands against the wall,” I order, and she slaps her palms down loudly against the brick behind her, one at each side of her legs.

Her chest rises and falls dramatically as her breathing increases. She keeps licking and biting her lips, her desperation showing. Why do women think this is a turn on? It’s not.

“You want a ride on the wild side?”

She nods, pushing her tits out at me. I’m a man, any release is better than no release.

“You wet for me?” I ask, and she giggles while nodding. “If you want me to get hard and stay hard, you don’t fucking make a sound. That giggling shit is annoying as fuck.”

Immediately, she snaps her mouth shut.

I yank her shirt up and pull her bra over her titties without unhooking it. Her nipples point out in the cold night air.

"You cold or is that for me?" I ask, flicking her nipple harshly.

"You," she whispers breathlessly.

I yank the waistband of her stretchy pants down, pulling her panties with them. Her curls glisten with her arousal under the street light.

With her pants at her ankles, I turn her around to face the wall. "Bend over, grab your ankles. You don't speak, don't touch me, and you don't move. If you want a wild ride with a biker, I'm gonna give you one you'll never forget."

While she positions herself, I grab a condom from my wallet and unbutton my four button jeans enough to release my cock. While stroking myself a few times to get fully erect, part of me considers just walking away. However, I'm a man with a dick, and pussy is pussy. No matter what my mood, it's a place to sink into for a time.

Covering myself carefully, I spread her ass cheeks and slide myself inside her slick cunt. The little whore is more than ready.

I close my eyes and picture a dark-haired beauty with ink covering her arms and a tight cunt made just for me. I can almost hear the gravelly voice of my dream woman as she moans my name, pushing back to take me deeper, thrust after thrust.

I roll my hips as the receptionist struggles to keep herself in position.

Raising my hand, I come down on the exposed globe of her ass cheek. "Dirty fucking girl." I spank her again. "I'm not your fucking daddy, but I'll give you what he obviously didn't." I spank her again and thrust. “Head down between your legs. Watch me fuck your pussy.”

She does as instructed and watches as I continue slamming into her. Stilling, I reach down and twist her nipples as she pushes back on me.

Her moans get louder as I move, gripping her hips and pistoning in and out of her.

I slap her ass again. “I said quiet.” Then I push deep, my hips hitting her ass, and she shakes as her orgasm overtakes her.

“Fuck me!” she wails.

I slam in and out, in and out, faster and faster, until I explode inside the condom.

She isn’t holding her ankles by the time I’m done. She’s still head down, bent over with her back against the wall as her hands hang limply like the rest of her body, trembling in aftershocks.

Pulling out, I toss the condom on the ground and walk away, buttoning my pants back up, no thought beyond washing her off me.

“Collector,” I hear X yell my road name from his doorway. “You ruined that one.” He nods to the bent over woman, smoking a cigarette and making it obvious he watched the show.

The noise has Judge coming to his door and giving me a nod of approval.

I look over my shoulder to see the bitch still hasn’t moved. Her pussy is out in the air, ass up, head down, and she’s still moaning. Desperate, needy, it’s not my thing.

“I need a shower,” I say, giving X a two finger salute before going into my own room where Deacon is already in bed and doesn't move as I go straight back to the shitty bathroom to clean up.

I wasn't lying. I smell like a bar, and now I smell the skank stench of easy pussy. I have needs, but I can't help wondering what it would be like to have to work for my release just once. It's not in my cards, though. Just like this town, this ride, and that broad, it's on to the next for me and my bothers of the Devil's Due MC.

Chapter Two

~Emerson~

"Well, I'll be damned," I hear Earl call from the front area of the shop. "Look what the cat drug in."

I start to make my way up front, pausing in the hallway at the side room that is my station.

"Long damn time, Old Dog," the sexy, gruff voice of a man replies.

My first thought is I need to get laid. If the mere sound of a man's voice has become sexy to me, then I have seriously gone too long between lovers. I don't need Mr. Right; I'm happy with Mr. Right Now.

"Dover Ragnes, what the devil are you doin' here?" Earl asks with noticeable pride in his voice.

My heart stops. In an instant, everything I thought I left behind in Tennessee has come full-force into the safety of my Alabama life. Out of all the places he could be, out of all the men who could come in that door, it would have to be the one man who ties me to the most helpless moment of my life.

Once upon a time, I could believe in fairytales. The days of dressing up in princess tiaras and plastic shoes left the day she did. Now I know the truth: happily ever after is only what you can make of the shit storm life gives you. Every breath is a treasured moment. In the blink of an eye, innocent lives are lost in the cruelest ways imaginable.

I have spent my entire life wishing on every star I could to turn back the hands of time. However, there is no fairy godmother to wave a wand, pot of gold at the end of a rainbow. Just like fairytales never do come true, neither does the one wish I would give everything for.

Raleigh believed in the stars, loved to gaze at them and make up her own names for each and every one. If only she had been right, then maybe my wish to bring her back would have come true.

"Passing through," Dover answers, and I keep myself hidden from his view. "How goes it, old timer?"

"It goes, young buck. It fucking goes. We doin' work for you, or you doin' work in the area?"

I back down the hallway of the tattoo shop that is covered in flash sheets set in frames for customers to choose from unless they want a custom piece. Continuing on, I pass by my station without going back in, as well as Randy's. I consider stopping in the piercing room and work on sanitizing tools, but then decide against it since the machine can be loud. I keep moving until I land myself in the back room. It's our supply room, break room, and Old Dog's office.

There is an old dining room table with four chairs back here in the middle of the room. The cabinets are filled with ink, towels, plastic wrap, and all our other supplies, as well as a few snacks for the days we don't have time to stop and eat a full meal. A fridge, microwave, and a sink line the wall. Earl has a desk in the back corner with a computer that may be one of the original models from the eighties going back to the old-school blinking black and green screen. Command-prompt garbage can is what he needs for that old clunker, but he uses it. His motto stands true in everything, including the computer: *if it ain't broke, don't fix it.*

I have no reason to be back here, but I can't be available if Dover needs work. No way, no how will I put my mark on his body, giving that piece of myself to him. Hell, he may not care, but that's my art on him forever.

My hands begin to tremble. He knows the reason my whole world changed when I was far too young to understand what she endured. He experienced the same loss, the fear that swept through the whole town, the reason my parents never again trusted me to be safe in our own home. He knows it all too well. He's the reason I spend night after night, even now, wishing I had something good to believe in. No, I cannot and will not ink him. Every time he would touch the tattoo, it would be touching something I created. There is no way I can be tied to Dover Ragnes like that, not with the history between us.

My mind goes back to her.

"Best friends forever and ever," Raleigh squeals as we ride our bikes down the quiet street of our neighborhood.

"Of course," I respond, pedaling faster and faster. Feeling brave, I let go of the handle bars.

Raleigh is the best bike rider I know. She wouldn't think twice about letting go and riding with her hands held high. Her older brother Dover taught her himself, and he's fearless. Now that he has his driver's license, he rides a motorcycle. It's loud, and he's always working on it, but he takes Raleigh to school on it if she misses the bus. He hasn't caught on that she misses the bus more often since he started taking her.

"You're doing it!" Raleigh encourages from my right side.

I smile from ear to ear. My best friend and I challenge ourselves together.

Boom. The hard ground seems to move up and crash with me instead of me falling to it. Everything happened so fast. One minute, I was free, and the next, I am on the ground.

Raleigh is over me in a flash. "Where does it hurt, Emerson?"

"Everywhere," I groan.

She lifts my hand and sees my wrist is bleeding. She doesn't miss a beat before taking the ribbon from her hair and wrapping it around and around.

"Better?" she asks.

I don't answer; I simply nod my head while the pain still runs through me. I don't want to tell her the ribbon didn't work. She never leaves home without a ribbon in her hair, always matching her outfit. She says it's like a girl's version of a super hero cape, and one day, she's going to have super powers to save the people she loves the most.

"I know it's not like mom's kisses or the special Band-Aids, but it'll have to do till we get home."

"Raleigh, you are the bestest ever. Thank you for sharing your ribbon with me."

"Dover says, 'It's not the fall that gets ya; it's the sudden stop.' I don't know exactly what that means, but stopping sure does hurt sometimes." She laughs, making me smile. Then she helps me off the ground and back onto my bike.

With the soft touch of my friend, the comfort of her aid, the pain subsides. We pedal as if we don't have a care in the world.

If only I would have known that would be our last bike ride together … Tracing the yellow bow tattooed in the form of the eternity symbol on the inside of my wrist, I think of her like I do a million times a day.

"Your big brother is all grown up, and he's here, Raleigh," I whisper to the space around me. My stomach burns. She should be here. Dammit, she should be here.

"Sonnie!" I hear Earl yell from the front.

I don't reply.

"Give me a second, fellas. I'll see if Sonnie has anything open tonight."

He doesn't wait for me to come to him; instead, Earl makes his way to where I am in the back as if I couldn't have heard him. It isn't long before the man who gave me a chance when I left everything I ever knew behind stands in front of me. Part of me wants to let it all tumble out of my mouth like the girl I am inside.

The woman I have grown into keeps quiet.

"Old Dog" is in his usual overalls with a black tank top under them. The old school markings in green and black ink cover him from his collarbone and shoulders all the way down to his wrists. His long, white beard goes down to his round beer belly. If he were to turn around, the white hair he sports is always in a braid that goes well beyond his shoulders. After his time in the service, he considers this his rebellion.

"For God and country" is tattooed down his right arm while *"For love and life"* is down his left arm as a tribute to all the things that have mattered most. The man is wise and loyal. From teaching me to sketch to allowing his leg to be my very first canvas, he has given me life through my art.

The man is almost seventy. He's seen war time and peace. He's seen mayhem and marked his story on his body as well as many others. Earl "Old Dog" Wilbur is a former Marine who is who he is and makes not one apology for it. He taught me my craft, gave me my start, and has been a father, friend, and the only family I really have left.

"You got time to squeeze in an old friend and his crew tonight?"

My eyes grow wide. I can't deny him anything when he gave me so much. I also know I can't go out there and see his eyes—her eyes—without getting lost in their depths.

"I'm not feeling so great, Old Dog," I try to pacify the situation.

"All right, darlin', go on home and get some rest." He comes over and gives my shoulder a squeeze.

Without giving myself away, I put my hand over his before I rise from the chair to leave. I don't look him in the eye as I grab my helmet and head toward the back door. I pause when I hear Earl start talking to the guys out front again.

"Sonnie ain't up to it tonight. My hands are bad now, boys. Come back tomorrow night if you're still in town; we'll get you fixed up."

Shit! Why didn't I think this through? Well, at least I have time to prepare myself for coming face to face with the memories I spent sixteen years fighting back.

Does he realize who Dover Ragnes is to me? Does he know the history between us? What does he know about the man he calls an old friend? In all the years I've spent with Earl, I don't remember a time when I have said Raleigh's name. He knows my parents sheltered me to the point I had to leave town or suffocate under them. However, never have I allowed myself to dive so deeply into my loss as to explain it to him.

I keep my bike parked right outside the backdoor of the shop. On the rainy days, it makes it easy to get in and out.

Sliding on my helmet, I climb on and start her up. The yellow and black Ninja comes to life under me as

I tuck down low to hug the curve as I round it, twisting the throttle.

Six Harleys are parked out front as I look in my mirrors and drive away. If only I could say for sure I was keeping Dover in my rear…

I still my mind from thoughts of my best friend's older brother as I look up at the starry night sky. Then I twist the throttle and grip the gas tank more firmly with my thighs as I feel the night air whip around me.

Getting home, I pull up to my back door. Earl helped me add a small lean-to off the porch for my bike. The tiny home lies on the end of a back road and is my sanctuary.

I hop off, dropping my helmet on the back stoop, and make my way inside. For the millionth time, I think to myself, *I should start locking up the place*. That's what sane, normal people do. Then I look around and realize I have nothing of value except my bike, and it's with me wherever I go.

My kitchen is directly through the backdoor. The stainless steel trim holds my Formica countertops in place. The white cabinets are what I call a retro feel, but it's more because the house was built in nineteen sixty-two, and it has not been updated. The yellow linoleum floor pops off the white of the cabinets, which I did take the time to repaint in a satin finish for shine. I only have a new stove and refrigerator because the original ones crapped out. I did go with stainless steel, only because they don't offer olive green anymore.

From the backdoor in the kitchen, I can see straight through to my front door. They call the style a shotgun house since a bullet could be fired from the front door and go straight through to the back uninterrupted. The label doesn't matter; it could be a shack for all I care. What's important is it's home. Since I left home, the last thing I ever want to feel again is trapped. The straight run through gives me the peace of mind that I can get out if I need to.

The bathroom is off the far corner of the kitchen, set diagonally from the back door. Since it's original, the bathtub and toilet are olive green against a blush pink tile. To most people, I'm probably crazy to live in the deep south and in this style of house; then add in my desire not to upgrade … Yeah, very few can understand. The colors may not work together, but they are together and have been a part of each person who has occupied this space's history. It means something.

Yeah, I have a problem with letting go. My innocence was lost when I was nine years old, and even though I only had her with me for a short time, I have carried her with me every day since. Just like the history in this house, I will hold onto it until I simply can't anymore.

My bedroom is no different than the style of the rest of the home. From the single bedroom on, the house is done in old, oak flooring that could use a stripping and refinishing. Then again, each scar holds its own story to tell.

My full-sized bed is against the wall long ways, as if it were a day bed without being one. I have my own style, and it's pretty much the opposite of whatever I feel like everyone else would do.

Passing through, I go to the living room. The walls are done in a sky blue, and the only furniture in the space is a bean bag chair and a lamp. I go to my salt water fish tank and feed my babies. They are all I have here that tie me down, and in the end, they are merely fish.

With my mind too amped up about what may or may not happen tomorrow, I forgo my usual reading and drawing time in the chair and decide to soak in a bath.

If only I could let my past go down the drain as easily as the water…

Read more in In the Red by Chelsea Camaron by clinking HERE

EXCERPT OF BOUND BY FAMILY BY RYAN MICHELE

Prologue

This life.

My life … is Ravage.

Some say it's my destiny. Others call this my curse.

Lucky for me, I don't give a fuck what anyone thinks. The man I've become is because of a choice—none of that other bullshit. Everyone in life has a choice, a path. What direction you take is up to you.

For me, I had this moment in my life, a moment when I knew who and what I'd become.

It wasn't forced or coerced as the talk has been around this small town. No, the moment that haunts my dreams is what created the man you see today.

Family.

From the beginning to the end, family is what you start with and what you end with. I'm bound to it, honored by it, and respected in it.

Chapter One

The echo of the hammer hitting bone crackles through the air in the small, dank room. The man's screams fill the space with pain, anger, and contempt. He doesn't want us here anymore than we want to be in this dump. Unfortunately for us both, he fucked up and it isn't an option. No, it's a necessity.

Fucking Stu.

Ravage Motorcycle Club, my family, we run a tight ship, so to speak. There is a code, rules of sorts that must be followed. Fall out of line, there will be punishment. Stu fell out of line.

Ryker laughs off to the side, pulling me away from my thoughts as I let go of the man's wrist, hammer still clenched in the other hand. The asshole, Stu, falls to his knees on the dirt floor, holding his broken finger.

That's not the only one he's going to get today for his stupidity.

He knows better. Everyone in Sumner, Georgia knows better. Hell, make that anyone who has ever heard of Ravage knows better.

"You've got a hell of a blow with that thing," Ryker calls out. The man is twisted and warped. He does this shit for fun and entertainment. Part of me thinks he gets off on it, but to each their own. Me, I do this shit out of duty and responsibility. Regardless, he's been by my side for years, and I wouldn't have it any other way.

When no response comes from me, Ryker walks up to the man and gives him a savage kick to the gut, making the man curl into a ball to protect himself.

Green and Jacks stand off to the side of the small space.

We brought Stu to one of our outbuildings. It's more like a rundown shack, but it has what we need to get the job done.

"I'm thinkin' we need to take off some piggies," Ryker eggs on, and a chuckle escapes me. He does have a way with words, saying exactly what he thinks with not an ounce of filter.

"Give me a shot," Jacks, another one of my brothers and a friend from high school, says as he holds his hand out to me, waiting for the hammer.

Handing it to him, I then take a step back and cross my arms. It's not me being a pussy. It's me wanting to get this shit done so we can get the fuck out of here.

"Money," I bark out to Stu as Ryker gives him another hard kick, this one to his thigh.

Stu owes our club fifty thousand seven hundred dollars and some change for merchandise he purchased. We gave him a week after the initial payment of fifty grand went smooth. Ravage and Stu have a history, and in that time, this is the first instance when Stu hasn't paid up in full. It'll be the last time as well.

"I-I can have it b-by the weekend," Stu stammers out as Jacks swings the hammer, hitting Stu in the ankle. Another crunching sound reverberates throughout the room.

Ryker smirks, coming to stand next to me and giving me a slight bump on the shoulder with his elbow. "Believe this fucker? Weekend?" He shakes his head and spits down at Stu. "Motherfucker, you have twenty-four hours to come up with the cash."

"If we don't have it by then, you're done," I add as Jacks takes another swing.

His cries of fear fill the air.

After an hour of making sure Stu gets the picture by using our fists and hammer, we ride.

~

Fresh air. The freedom of feeling the elements surround me. The delicate balance of navigating a road or eating asphalt.

It's the best part of every day.

The ride.

My bike is a beauty. A Heritage Softtail Harley painted black and red—Ravage MC colors. Working on her has been my pastime for years, tuning and cleaning. I take care of her, and she takes care of me. Wouldn't have it any other way. There's something about taking garbage and turning it into something you love. That's my bike. She began as a pile of shit and turned out to be absolutely perfect.

Life ties us down. Materials hold people back. The open road is about freedom. Ravage is freedom. We live to our code, our standards, and we take care of our own.

My mind clears on the open road awaiting me, nothing but blacktop and paint ahead. Riding allows me the peaceful time to think. Sometimes my rides last hours, while others only last minutes. Normally, whenever my mind figures out what it needs to, that's the time I pull my bike to a stop.

Lately, the Ravage MC has been bringing in some serious money with all the deals that Pops has worked out over the years. Some of them bring more than others, but it's becoming more difficult to filter the money. Especially with the amount of cash. There's only so much we can put through the garage and Studio X, the strip club. Even Stu owes us, and when that cash shows up … Well, it's got to go somewhere.

It's been working well, but we had to stock pile cash in several of our vaults in the clubhouse basement. Having cash on hand is great in the times we need it, but it will continually increase over time if we keep at this pace. That being said, we need something else to funnel the money.

The thing is, I've been around the club my whole life. I prospected in early. Just turning twenty-two, I've held my place for four years now. I'm ready to step up anywhere needed. More so, I'm ready to give a fresh mindset and view to the way we do business. It's all for family.

My Ravage family.

My top idea is a car wash. It's an all-cash business, unless you let the customers use credit cards, which I would advise against. If we keep it all cash, we could put some of the money through there. I even searched the internet about all the working parts of one of the machines and how much it would take to build and maintain it. Ravage could easily do it, but the downside is all the moving pieces. Sure, we can go and fix the shit, but I want to work smarter, not harder.

There's a way, and I will damn well find it.

My parents taught me many things. The first and foremost is to be my own man. If that means carving a new path for the Ravage MC, I'm up to the task.

~

Pulling up to the clubhouse, we park in the lot, all next to each other, turning off the engines and taking off our helmets.

This building is home.

My memory is damn good, which is both a blessing and a curse. My father doesn't know, but I remember living with my biological mother and seeing stuff as a young child that was flat-out wrong. It's not that he doesn't care to know; we just don't talk about it.

Besides, remembering those times only pisses me off. Seeing men come in and out of the small apartment, going into that woman's bedroom then coming out a while later. She was always doped up on something. Back then, I thought she just wasn't feeling well.

When she started hitting me, that was when I knew what fear was. A woman is supposed to love their kid, at least somewhat. Mine didn't. Not at all.

The moment my father told that woman—my incubator, as we call her now—I was staying with him, that's what I consider my rebirth. It was a new start. Not only that, but I had a new mother, as well.

One who loved me, took care of me, and put all my needs above anyone else's, not giving two shits what anyone thought about it.

When I started living, this ugly-as-fuck, cement-blocked building became home. Don't get me wrong, we had a house, as well, but the clubhouse is where it all started for me.

"How'd it go?" Pops, the president of Ravage MC and my grandfather, asks upon us entering the building as I get chin lifts from the guys.

Pops has been the president since I came to Ravage—at least eighteen years. He's done a great job building the Ravage Motorcycle Club into very profitable entities. Not only that, after the bullshit that went down when I was a kid, Pops keeps a tight leash on any and all our friends and enemies. One doesn't do what we do and not have a huge basket of both, but Pops has kept it all in line.

"Ryker got a little too happy, so the guy won't be having kids, probably ever, but the message was sent. If he doesn't have it by the weekend, then we'll take care of it."

Pops chuckles.

"Hey, the fucker was tryin' to stand up. If he would've stayed down, his nuts wouldn't have cracked."

Laughter is heard throughout the clubhouse.

Pops slaps his hand on my shoulder, giving it a squeeze. The look he gives me is different, but he says nothing as he walks to one of the tables and has a seat.

I've noticed things about him these last few months. The looks that come across his face when he thinks no one is looking, as if he's tired and the weight of the world rests on his shoulders. There's no doubt in my mind that it's true.

Running an entire MC is a shit-ton of work. Even doing it for years and having it down pat, there comes a time when it could be too much. I kept my mouth shut about it, though, not wanting to overstep my boundaries. When Pops is ready to tell us what's going on, he will.

Heading toward the bar, I grasp the cold beer sitting on it then join the guys at the table. Blood means nothing to any of us. We are a family of our own choosing. Each one of us couldn't be more different if we tried. It's as if we were put together in this clubhouse for a reason.

Take Becs. He's the vice president and has recently told us that he'd like to step down and let one of the younger guys take his role. That decision is huge and one of the highest topics at our next church. Becs is quiet. Silent but deadly. He's never up in your face, but one wrong move, and he will tear you down.

Then there's Rhys. He's silent, but his face, body—hell, even the air around him—screams "breath my air, and I'll end you."

My dad, Cruz, he's middle road between the two. He has no problem getting in someone's face, yet he'll only do it when necessary. His face isn't scary like Rhys', but he has his own badass vibe he puts off.

Me, I'm more of a thinker, a planner if you will. I like to look at all the possibilities and facts before coming up with a strategy.

Somehow, all our crazy asses fit together, and we are bound by family.

Find out more in *Bound by Family* by clicking HERE

ABOUT CHELSEA CAMARON

USA Today bestselling author Chelsea Camaron is a small town Carolina girl with a big imagination. She's a wife and mom, chasing her dreams. She writes contemporary romance, erotic suspense, and psychological thrillers. She loves to write about blue-collar men who have real problems with a fictional twist. From mechanics to bikers to oil riggers to smokejumpers, bar owners, and beyond she loves a strong hero who works hard and plays harder.

Join Chelsea in Chelsea's Biker Broads FB Group

Chelsea can be found on social media at

www.authorchelseacamaron.com

chelseacamaron@gmail.com

OTHER BOOKS BY CHELSEA CAMARON

Love and Repair Series: Available in KU

Crash and Burn

Restore My Heart

Salvaged

Full Throttle

Beyond Repair

Stalled

Box Set Available

Hellions Ride Series:

One Ride

Forever Ride

Merciless Ride

Eternal Ride

Innocent Ride

Simple Ride

Heated Ride

Ride with Me (Hellions MC and Ravage MC Duel with Ryan Michele)

Originals Ride

Final Ride

Roughneck Series: Available in KU

Maverick

Heath

Lance

Box Set Available

Stand Alone Thriller – Stay

Stand Alone Short Romances – Serving My Soldier

Mother Trucker

Devil's Due MC Series:

Crossover

In The Red

Below The Line

The following series are co-written

The Fire Inside Series:

(co-written by Theresa Marguerite Hewitt)

Kale

Regulators MC Series:

(co-written by Jessie Lane)

Ice

Hammer

Coal

Summer of Sin Series

Original Sin (co-written with Ripp Baker, Daryl Banner, Angelica Chase, MJ Fields, MX King)

Caldwell Brothers Series

(co-written by USA Today Bestselling Author MJ Fields)

Hendrix

Morrison

Jagger

Stand Alone Romance – co-written with MJ Fields

Visibly Broken

Use Me

Ruthless Rebels MC Series – co-written with Ryan Michele)

Shamed

Scorned

Scarred

Schooled

ABOUT RYAN MICHELE

Ryan Michele found her passion in bringing fictional characters to life. She loves being in an imaginative world where anything is possible, and she has a knack for special twists readers don't see coming.

She writes MC, Contemporary, Erotic, Paranormal, New Adult, Inspirational, and other romance-based genres. Whether it's bikers, wolf-shifters, mafia, etc., Ryan spends her time making sure her heroes are strong and her heroines match them at every turn. When she isn't writing, Ryan is a mom and wife living in rural Illinois and reading by her pond in the warm sun.

Join Ryan's Sultry Sinners Group on Facebook

Come Find Me

www.authorryanmichele.net

ryanmicheleauthor@gmail.com

OTHER BOOKS BY RYAN MICHELE

Ravage MC Series

Ravage Me

Seduce Me

Consume Me

Inflame Me

Captivate Me

Ravage MC Novella Collection

Ride with Me (co-written with Chelsea Camaron)

Ravage MC Bound Series

Bound by Family

Bound by Desire

Bound by Vengeance

Vipers Creed MC Series

Challenged

Conquering

Conflicted (Coming soon)

Ruthless Rebels MC Series (co-written with Chelsea Camaron)

Shamed

Scorned

Scarred

Schooled

Loyalties Series

Blood & Loyalties: A Mafia Romance

Raber Wolf Pack Series

Raber Wolf Pack Book 1

Raber Wolf Pack Book 2

Raber Wolf Pack Book 3

Stand Alone Romances

Full Length Novels

Needing to Fall

Safe

Wanting You

Short Stories

Hate to Love

Branded

Novellas

Billionaire Romance Series

Stood Up

DON'T MISS A RELEASE!

Come join Chelsea Camaron and Ryan Michele in our groups on Facebook

Chelsea Camaron

Ryan Michele

Want to be up to date on all New Releases? Sign up for our Newsletter

Chelsea Camaron

Ryan Michele